George Corfe

Man and his many changes, or Seven times seven
Second Edition

ISBN/EAN: 9783337107994

Printed in Europe, USA, Canada, Australia, Japan

Cover: Foto ©Raphael Reischuk / pixelio.de

More available books at **www.hansebooks.com**

George Corfe

Man and his many changes, or Seven times seven

Second Edition

MAN

AND HIS MANY CHANGES

OR, SEVEN TIMES SEVEN.

BY

GEORGE CORFE, M.D.

M.R.C.P. (LOND.);

PHYSICIAN TO THE WESTERN GENERAL DISPENSARY, AND LATE SENIOR
RESIDENT MEDICAL OFFICER AT THE MIDDLESEX HOSPITAL.

SECOND EDITION.

LONDON:

HOULSTON AND WRIGHT
65, PATERNOSTER ROW.
MDCCCLXII.

PREFACE.

In sitting down to write a book, however small, the author ought to have one object in view, viz., the benefit of his fellow-man. In the course of the writer's professional experience of thirty years, he has found the greatest ignorance existing in the minds of in-telligent parents on the dietetic method of managing their children; in other words, people know not on what to feed, how much to feed, or when to feed, their little ones, if in delicate health, or before disease compels them to seek medical help and instruction. This ignorance is not only exhibited in parents towards their offspring: but also in well-informed persons towards themselves, many of whom will indulge in food or in drink, which is so far prejudicial, that the ill-effect is not betrayed until the doctor is called to the sick bed, to witness the result of imprudence, in the struggles of some painful malady. The education of youth has made great advances within this quarter of a century—witness our "Ragged Schools," "Infant Nurseries," "Homes," &c.; but how very little has been done for the instruction of parents in the mode of feeding and nurturing their children. The reasoning of all classes is pretty much the same on this subject. If a glass of spirits comforts the stomach of the mother, surely it will do the same for the puny child. If beef and dumplings satisfy a father's appetite, the same must satisfy that of the baby; though it has not a tooth to gnaw, much less to grind, either; and then the mother wonders that it cries at night, and will not suck by day. Overdosing with sweets will effectually bring on nursery sorrows, such as mal-assimilation of food, sickliness of stomach, and weakness of body.

The facts here recorded have been noted down during the author's "odd moments," snatched from an active professional life, during which period he has had upwards of 375,000 fellow-creatures, the subjects of disease and suffering, pass under his notice. From this vast field, the difficulty has consisted in selecting materials for so small a brochure, rather than in being at a loss, from a scarcity of matter, for illustration. The writer has endeavoured, like an artist, to sketch a few portraits of disease; and though he is aware that they are imperfect, yet he craves the forbearance of the professional reader, and begs him to examine the subjects treated of, before he condemns the premises.

To the general reader, he would remark that a sincere desire to throw some light and afford information on the domestic management of several diseases under our control, has actuated him in writing these pages; and if he succeeds in this feeble attempt, he will be amply repaid, and would gratefully acknowledge the debt as due to Him "from whom cometh every good and every perfect gift," and in Whom we both "live, and move, and have our being."

9, NOTTINGHAM TERRACE,
    REGENT'S PARK, N.W.

CONTENTS.

FOURTH STAGE—YOUNG MEN TO MEN.

TWENTY-ONE TO TWENTY-EIGHT YEARS.

FIFTH STAGE—MEN.

TWENTY-EIGHT TO FORTY-NINE YEARS.

SIXTH STAGE—ELDERLY MEN.

FORTY-NINE TO SEVENTY YEARS.

SEVENTH STAGE—OLD MEN.

SEVENTY TO NINETY-EIGHT YEARS.

CONCLUDING ADVICE AND REMARKS.

INTRODUCTION.

In passing through one of the streets near Covent Garden, this summer, the writer's eye was arrested by a singularly old-fashioned picture, in the window of a respectable bookseller. It proved to be a fac-simile of a curious print, found by Mr. Winter Jones on the manuscript of N. de Lyra's "Moralia super Bibliam," in the British Museum.

This singular print, supposed by Mr. Jones to belong to the 15th century, has in its left corner a cradle, with an infant, and a label, "Generacio," upon it. At the foot of the cradle stands a boy, naked, who appears to be holding out his hands, and amusing the infant by clapping them. The next figure, ascending the left side of the print, is a naked child, with a toy known as a windmill, and underneath, on a scroll, are the words, "An infant to 7 years." Above this is an inscription, "Childhood to 15 years," represented by a youth, holding a falcon in his right hand, and a bag of money in his left: emblems of the love of pleasure and enjoyment natural to this stage of man's life. Above the head of the youth there is another label, "Adolescence to 25 years." This brings us to the top of the left-hand side. In the centre, at the upper part of the print, and sitting astride upon a wheel, is a figure with a feather in his cap, armed with spear and shield. A label above says "Youth to 35 years." At the top of the right side is another label, "Manhood to 50 years." Beneath is a figure at a table, counting money, evidently the worldly man, who, having passed through the stages

B

of pleasure and war, is now occupied with the acquisition of wealth. Under him are the words, " Old age to 70 years." The next figure is an old man leaning on a staff, with the inscription, " Decrepit until death." The dead body is next represented, lying in a coffin, under which is a label, with the word " Corrupcio."

A figure with expanded wings and flowing drapery occupies the foot of the print, the hands resting on the two labels, " Generacio," and " Corrupcio."

Eight lines are added in monkish Latin, which the editor has thus rendered :—

> " The state of man is exemplified in a flower :
> The flower falls and perishes—so shall man, also, become ashes.
> If thou could'st know who thou art, and whence thou comest,
> Thou wouldst never smile, but ever weep.
> There are three things which often make me lament :
> First, it is a hard thing to know that I must die ;
> Secondly, I fear, because I do not know when I shall die ;
> Thirdly, I weep, because I do not know what will become of me
> hereafter."

The writer of the following pages had long been desirous of recording some general facts connected with the disorders of man's sevenfold state, and, on seeing this curious print, he resolved that a notice of it should form the subject of some introductory remarks.

Both Heathens, Jews, and Christians, from the earliest periods, have divided man's life into ten or seven stages. The latter division has always found most favour with modern anatomists and physiologists. A Jewish writer of the ninth century remarks, " that the preacher's seven vanities are seven worlds, through which man has to pass." But the great founder of medicine, Hippocrates, makes the observation, that " in the nature of man, he has to pass through seven periods, called ages—1, the infant ; 2, the boy ; 3, the youth ; 4, the young man ; 5, the man ; 6, the elder man ; 7, the aged man. For the infant is within seven years, until he puts forth his teeth ; the boy until puberty, at twice seven years ; the youth until the growth of his beard, at thrice seven years; the young man up to four times seven, until the whole body is grown; the man up to forty-nine; the elderly man to fifty-six, or eight times seven; whatever is beyond this belongs to old age."

These ages, stages, or periods, or by whatever title we call them, are really so many different epochs in our life, during which the pleasures, toils, diseases, pursuits, &c., are as different and as peculiar as are the habits of one animal from another. The busy bee is not more opposite in character to the tardy, ursine sloth, than are the energetic habits of the young enterprising man to those of the decrepit octogenarian.

But we need not search ancient writings to substantiate a fact well known amongst us all. The physiologist will tell you, that though our bodies appear to us unchanged since yesterday, yet they have, within these few hours, cast off countless decomposed particles, and these have been replaced by others. We fancy ourselves at rest, and yet a torrent of blood is propelled, moment by moment, by an indefatigable heart, and flows constantly through all our arteries and veins—a restless, and yet ever-renewed current—down to the grave. The very insignificant fall of one hair is preceded by decomposition of its bulb; and the autumnal sere leaf does not drop until its hold on the stem has previously become a mass of decomposed tissue.

But now let us view man from his conception to his birth, and we find that he passes through nine months, or seven times forty days; from birth to his seven months farther he is a sucking babe, and now shows his first teeth; whilst four times seven (or 2¼ years) brings him to the full cutting or development of his whole twenty teeth, and thus ends man's first stage of seven years.

At the entrance into his second stage of another seven years, he begins to cut his permanent teeth: first his molars, or double teeth; then his front; then the bicuspides, or half-double; then the canine; and all these several teeth come forth from their primitive bed in pairs, with as much periodical regularity, in a healthy child, as the seasons succeed each other. Irregularity here, as in Nature's operations elsewhere, is disorder or disease.

From the second to the third stage, other processes of development are going on towards maturing the man, until he arrives at his prime—four times seven years; and thus he continues until seven times seven, when he may be said to have ceased to build up the fabric, and age now gradually takes down what adolescence had previously raised; and thus we have a distinct series of stages marked out in man's eventful life, so that, without any strain of the imagination, we may fairly represent this life thus:—

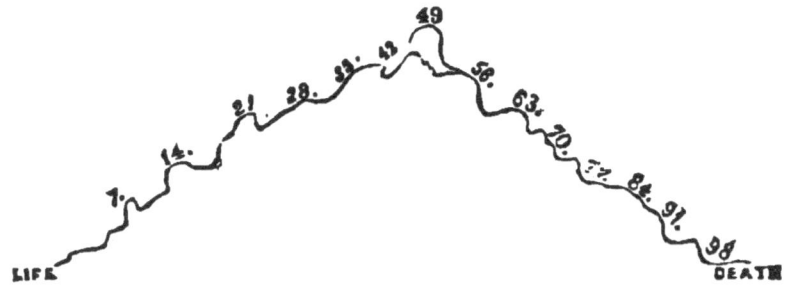

How appropriate is the remark that we begin to die as soon as we are born! But, to the Christian, the transition is one of joy and endless peace, when he can say—

"Life is the road to death,
Yet death life's gate must be;
Since heaven 's the throne of Christ,
And Christ is life to me."

5

FIRST STAGE.

INFANCY TO CHILDHOOD.

ONE TO SEVEN YEARS.

CHAPTER I.

Cycles of Life in the Vegetable and Animal Kingdoms—Lactation; its
blessings and evils—Errors in Infant Feeding—Croup.

"Perpetual motion and change," writes Dr. Hartwig, "is the
grand law, to which the whole of the created universe is subject,
and immutable stability is nowhere to be found but in the Eternal
Mind that rules and governs all things: 'He is in one mind, who
can turn Him?'"

One of the most beautiful evidences of the all-creating power and
wisdom of God is to be met with in the well-known fact that our
growth perfectly harmonizes with our wants. If the sucking child
required beef and mutton to support it at birth, this Power would
have supplied it with front teeth to gnaw, and double teeth to grind
such food; instead of which, the babe requires the rudiments or
elements of bone rather than muscle, and these elements abound in
the maternal milk, but gradually disappear after the seventh to the
fourteenth month of suckling, when they are scarcely to be met
with. Now higher and stronger powers are required; the teeth
and muscle must be fully developed, and the elements for their
formation are to be met with in the "staff of life," pure corn flour,

and vegeto-animal juices as food ; and thus we might go on to trace
the perfect adaptation of internal structures to the requirements of
our species in the several stages of life.   This beautiful harmony is
noticed in the vegetable, as well as in this, the animal kingdom.   As
there are epochs, or periods, in vegetation, so there are hours for
flowering ; for, though plants, like man, accommodate themselves to
the climate in which they grow and flower at certain seasons, yet,
when transferred to other climates, where the seasons are reversed,
they still have a tendency to flower at their accustomed period of
the year.   The great botanist, Linnæus, noticed the periodicity of
many flowers to expand at certain hours of the day; and, from this
fact, he constructed a floral clock, which marked, at different
hours, the expansion of certain flowers.   There is some mysterious
yet wise law in this arrangement throughout Nature's operations.
It is well-known that the ages of trees may be ascertained by the
number of the concentric circles in their trunks, each circle, in
particular trees (exogenous) denoting a year in age.   At the period
when a tree is in its prime, it then forms the largest circle or zone.
In the oak, this is said to be when between thirty and forty years of
age.   If we glance at the formation of the inhabitants of the waters,
we may determine the age of a fish by a microscopical examination
of its scales ; the concentric rings are supposed to afford the same
information which appears in the transverse section of a tree; and
in fishes void of scales (as the skate), rings, on the connecting
surfaces of the back bone, are believed to give similar evidence as to
the age of the fish.   These facts, with very many others, are
brought forward merely to show that the law of periodicity—the
law of cycle—is the basis of Nature's grand operations in vegetable
and in animal life.   As these periods pass on from one to another,
that is, from life to death, highly important changes take place in
the animal frame, in order that each successive change should
harmonize with those wants which arise from increasing years.

Each stage, also, of man's eventful life, brings with it so many
especial diseases, though each disease is peculiar to the period of his
life, and may therefore be termed periodical diseases, thus—measles,

whooping-cough, and scarlet-fever, are looked upon as infantile disorders; whilst gout is the trouble of man in the prime of life; and palsy the breaking up of the aged man's constitution.

It is proposed, therefore, to treat of the diseases which occur in periodical spaces of time, from the cradle to the grave, and to give some practical hints, by which parents may, with God's blessing, alleviate these evils when medical advice is not readily to be obtained.

Let us, in the first place, make a few remarks on the management of a baby. No woman, much less one who professes to be a Christian mother, has the smallest ground for refusing to suckle her offspring, and to give it that inestimable boon which God has furnished her with, for the sustenance, comfort, and growth of her helpless babe, namely, the maternal milk. Necessity alone can plead as an excuse, such as inflamed breasts, or a deficiency of milk from debility or constitutional causes, so that nursing would endanger the life of the parent. A mother is no more justified in entrusting the care of her babe to a wet-nurse, than she is in denying herself her own daily sustenance. It is in the highest degree a moral obligation, on her part, to give her offspring the parental milk, for 9 months at least, and, at the expiration of that time, to commence weaning it by degrees. The best time to give the infant suck is about the 4th hour after meals, when the milk contains more nourishing materials, as the digestion is then nearly completed. If the mother go 8 or 10 hours without food, the milk becomes yellowish, and even nauseous, and is often spit out by the infant. It is calculated that 2 lbs. of milk are obtained from 6 lbs. of meat consumed by the mother. From the period of birth till about the 14th week there is really nothing to remark; but about this time the rash of "red gum" usually appears, caused by "breeding the teeth." The structure of these rudimentary masticators, buried in the infantile jaws, their evolution at distinct and marked periods, their symmetrical arrangement in pairs, the growth of the teeth themselves, their changes to maturity and then decay in the first set and their replacement by another, present a train of mysterious, yet

wonderful operations, in which the mind is lost in contemplation.
This "breeding" time may be known by the looseness with which
the infant grasps the nipple, and the frequency with which it lets go
its hold, accompanied with fretfulness, and succeeded by copious
discharge of clear water (saliva) from its mouth.   The excited
irritability of the gums is deadened by biting any hard substance.
It is important at this period that the maternal milk should be free
from acidity; for an excess of vegetable food, or an indulgence in
potatoes, bottled ales, wine, or spirits, will tend to irritate the
infant's stomach, by an increase of acid in the milk, and thus the
nervous excitement may run on to the production of startings in
sleep, dry cough, relaxed bowels, and even convulsions and death.
The weaning time at length arrives, and with it, perhaps, three or
more pair of teeth.   This is a period of the greatest importance to
the health of the infant   It is no exaggeration to state, that from
the writer's long experience amongst the children of the humbler
classes in this great metropolis, he finds that three-fifths, at least, die
under two years of age, from ill feeding or over feeding, rather than
from *want* of food.

It is a common error to suppose that a farinaceous diet should be
substituted for the maternal milk.   Light animal broths thickened
with flour, pearl barley, rice or vermicelli, custard, batter, and
other puddings, with the moderate use of bread, or, what is far
better, unfermented or milk biscuits and honey, treacle or butter
in succession, compose the healthiest form of diet for weaned infants
until the dentition is completed.   A few hours ago I was summoned
to see a nurse child 15 months old : it was plump, rosy, and,
apparently, to an unprofessional eye, in rude health; but a rough
state of the skin of the face and forehead told its own tale : the
child had for months been fed on bread, potatoes, arrowroot, and
such like starchy food, with the addition of that extraordinary compound known as London skim-milk.   An east wind set in a few
days ago, and the child became husky, and wheezed.   That formidable disease croup had now developed itself, and, in spite of the
most active measures, the little sufferer died from suffocation in the

course of the night. This is one of a thousand of such cases—the result of ill-feeding. It may be here remarked, that those children who are over-fed with starchy and farinaceous substances, though they plump up, yet they are oftener the victims of croup than the more delicate, puny ones, who refuse much of the food which the others eat with avidity.

FIRST STAGE.

INFANCY TO CHILDHOOD.

ONE TO SEVEN YEARS.

CHAPTER II.

Milk and Flour; their composition, use and importance in Infancy—Bone Formation—Weaning; its troubles and disorders—Flesh Formation—Moulting in Man.

IT has been truly stated by that eminent investigator of the food we eat and of the fluids we drink, Dr. Prout, in his celebrated work on " the Stomach," that milk may be taken as the type of human food. He divided food into four groups :—The aqueous, the saccharine, the albuminous, and the oleaginous. In the first, we have water, tea, coffee, &c., &c. In the second, such articles as sugar, sweet fruits, arrowroot, sago.* In the third, are comprehended " fish, flesh and fowl," and also cheese ; and, lastly, the oil group, containing 70 to 80 per cent. of carbon, represented by butter, animal fats, &c., &c. Now, as milk really shadows forth the character of all the food of which we partake, and as it should enter very largely into the nourishing material for children, it cannot be out of place to introduce some observations at the commencement of the first

* It should be borne in mind that the two last are starchy subtances, and by digestion are converted into saccharine matter.

stage of Infantile Life, on the composition, action and uses of milk in the animal economy. We will not attempt a scientific analysis of the subject, a well-known fact is the following:—The young of all mammalia, or sucking animals, feed on this important compound for several months (many of them above a year), and get no other diet; yet they grow rapidly, and increase in size and are in health, consequently they have derived all the constituents of their muscle, nerve, bone, skin, hair, nay every tissue, from the milk they have taken as food. A pound weight of cow's milk contains a large proportion of group the first; namely, 1, water ($\frac{5}{8}$); 2, some sugar ($\frac{3}{4}$ oz.); 3, the flesh-forming or cheesy principle, caseine ($\frac{3}{4}$ oz.); and, lastly, the fat or oily matter is represented by the butter of which there is ($\frac{1}{2}$ oz.). In some countries, the milk of the goat is the popular diet, just as cow's milk is employed in our islands. There are many instances, also, in which recourse is had to asses' milk, and it is of some importance, therefore, that we should have a general and correct idea of the composition of this invaluable article of children's food; thus:—

	Human Milk, 1 lb.; contains.		Cow's Milk, 1 lb.; contains.		Asses' Milk, 1 lb.; contains,	
	ozs.	grs.	ozs.	grs.	ozs.	grs.
1. Water . . .	14 —	41	13 —	333	14 —	76
2. Sugar . . .	0 —	280	0 —	315	0 —	420
3. Caseine . .	0 —	210	0 —	350	0 —	140
4. Butter . . .	0 —	210	0 —	245	0 —	105

Besides these principles, each contains a small proportion of mineral matters: such as phosphates of lime, potash, and a trace of iron; these ingredients being required especially for the building up of the bony fabric. Let me here revert to the wondrous fact, that the nearer the female approaches to the period of parturition, the more is the milk charged with phosphates of lime, and it is not till the digestive organs of the infant are sufficiently strengthened to be enabled to appropriate this salt from other food, that it ceases to appear in the maternal milk. The same ingredient is always found in the urine of adults, but not in the urine of infants. The rapid formation of the bones, in the early stages of life, requires that there should be no waste of any of these foundation elements of the skeleton—the phosphoric salts; and nature has provided accordingly.* Blush ye infidels at these overpowering facts, if ye fail to acknowledge the Almighty finger of Design and Harmony,—of Wisdom and Goodness—in such an inscrutable chain of demand and supply in the rise, progress, and completion of this frail body, our mortal tenement! What an inexhaustible store-house is the Boundless Treasury of Nature!

This valued animal salt exists also in the farina of wheat. It has been estimated by eminent chemists that a person who eats a pound of farina a day, will swallow 3 lbs., 6 ozs., 4 drs., and 44 grs. of phosphate of lime in the year. It is a curious fact, by-the-by, that wheat *straw*, which was not intended for the food of man, contains carbonate of lime and not phosphate. Shells of birds' eggs also contain phosphate of lime; and the young, before hatching, consume this salt for the purpose of forming its bones, hence the shell becomes thinner and thinner as the hatching period arrives, so that the unfledged inhabitant has no difficulty in bursting through its tiny house of half consumed lime, to " pick up " its own independent sustenance.

Towards the 7th month, and earlier in some mothers, the milk begins to fail, or at least to be insufficient for the sustenance of the infant, and it is of the utmost importance to know what substitute should be adopted in lieu of the maternal milk. Asses' milk is most allied to human milk in its sugar, caseine, and butter principles; though cow's milk contains more of the flesh-giving material, and therefore more cream and cheese and less water; namely, caseine. A very good practice is the following :—to every pint of cow's milk, add half-a-pint of water, and a small quantity of sugar ,

---

* " The fat of the kidneys of wheat," though a highly figurative expression, contains a depth of meaning. In the wheat exists all the nourishment essential to man.

and thus reduced, it approaches sufficiently near to human milk for all healthy purposes. The great cause of infant mortality in London arises from the inability to obtain cow's milk sweet, fresh and genuine. The smell of fresh-drawn milk is peculiar: it sinks in water, but floats in blood. If it be good, a drop put on the finger nail flows slowly down, not unlike a globule of thin oil. But soon after milk is drawn from the cow it undergoes decomposition, and it has been observed that the infant mortality in the metropolis is usually greatest during the intense hot months, for, as this increase of temperature gives rise to sour cow's milk, bowel disorders and death are the usual consequences of its administration. If lime-water, in the proportion of a table-spoonful to every quarter of a pint be added, this acidity may be arrested in a great measure. But the evil lies deeper still, the cows are kept in close sheds in the heart of this great city; they are fed on grains, soured by heat and exposure after the alcohol or beer is extracted, or they are indulged with an occasional feed of swedes, mangold-wurzel, carrots, turnips, &c., and the result is an abundance of thin milk, which has a tendency to pass rapidly into an acid state, and this milk has to be farther diluted by the addition of water, or some adulteration worse than all.

As I have already hinted, it is not natural that an infant, under 7 or 9 months old, should be fed on anything but its mother's milk, though, after that period, we may add a small quantity of farinaceous food, of which the most important, because the most nutritious, is pure wheat flour. Every pound of this " staff of life " contains 2 ozs. 21 grs. of a substance which resembles muscle or flesh, and hence it is a powerful " flesh former ;" in addition to which, an ingredient is found in it that does not exist either in barley or oats, viz., albumen, of which, the white of an egg is a per-fect specimen. This important agent serves to build up the infantile brain and nerves, or to repair the constant loss of this matter during our manhood growth ; and thus, in milk and in wheat we have all the elements for animal sustenance and increase, for we are in a state of perennial moult. Crabs and lobsters throw off their shell altogether ; birds, their feathers ; and horses, their hair ; but, in the human being, we find this process of moulting going on constantly —our skin rubs off, our mucous membrane wears away, and our internal organs all of them disappear by a similar process ; so that an eminent lecturer once calculated that " a human being loses about the 40th part of his weight every day, and that the vital organs of the human body are renewed every 40 days."

FIRST STAGE.

INFANCY TO CHILDHOOD.

ONE TO SEVEN YEARS.

CHAPTER III.

Dentition; its pains and diseases—Convulsions—Perfection of Infantile Hearing—Infant Schools and Amusements—Cleanliness of Skin and Purity of Air essential to Health.

As the whole process of dentition is so intimately connected with the healthy growth of the child, it would be well if mothers made themselves thoroughly conversant with the operations of Nature, and narrowly watched this process from month to month. Convulsions, tardiness of speech, stuttering, which may merge into confirmed stammering, periodical headaches, imperfect digestion, wasting, and capricious bowels, are a few of the disorders arising from imperfect dentition.

What is the period of life at which the teeth should be cut? my readers may inquire.

To establish this period correctly would be a most difficult matter. As society is now constituted, circumstances tend to surround the subject with insuperable obstacles so as to adjust the correct time, though it may be generally said to vary from the 6th to the 8th month, for the first eruption. The teeth usually appear in pairs. The two lower front ones should be first; then, after a short period, say 20 days, the two upper ones; these are succeeded by the lateral couple of front teeth (incisors) in the lower jaw; then follow also a similar two in the upper jaw. The lower jaw next throws up its two molar teeth that lie nearest to the lateral incisors last seen; then follows the same eruption in the upper jaw. After which the lower canines (dog teeth) appear; then the upper canines; lastly, the two second sets of molars of the lower jaw, followed by the corresponding sets of molars of the upper jaw.

UPPER JAW.

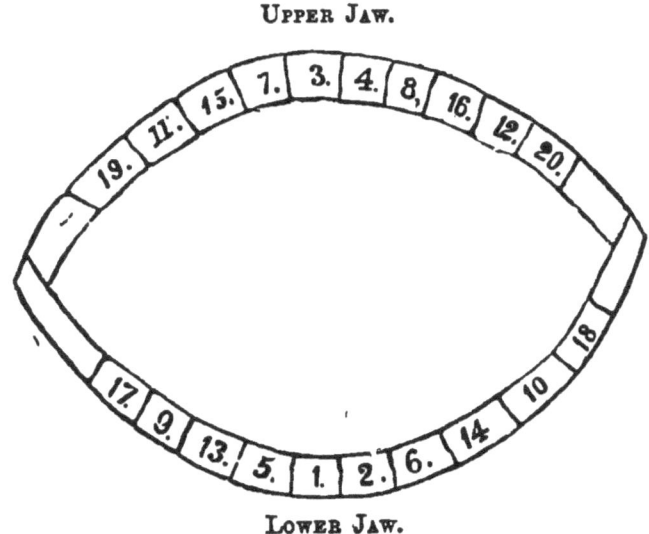

LOWER JAW.

Or, thus :—

Periods.		Teeth.		
7 months	..	Two central incisors,	lower	jaw
8 ,,	..	Two ,, ,,	upper	,,
9 ,,	..	Two lateral ,,	lower	,,
10 ,,	..	Two ,, ,,	upper	,,
12 or 14 months ..		Two molars ,,	lower	,,
15 ,, 17 ,,	..	Two ,, ,,	upper	,,
18 to 20 ,,	..	Two canine ,,	lower	,,
20 ,, 22 ,,	..	Two ,, ,,	upper	,,
22 ,, 30 ,,	..	Two molar ,,	lower	,,
— ,, — ,,	..	Two ,, ,,	upper	,,

There is no circumstance relating to youth more striking than the division of life into epochs. The climacteric years of the ancients were multiples of seven, and they were pretty accurate observers of the changes which took place in the body at differents periods. That there must be a rule, regulating the grand epochs of development in a perfectly healthy individual, there can be no doubt. In the course of life, man appears, in the changes to which his frame is subjected, to go through several types of configuration. The same individual that had once, in the womb of his parent, a shapeless form, and became an infant, breathing air, is by no means to be recognized as identical with the vigorous man of 35. His physiognomy alone points out the changes effected upon him, and we cannot doubt that there must be some ground for the vulgar observation that has come down to us, of the body undergoing remarkable changes during the course of successive climacterics. The circumstances relating to dentition are but an isolated set of phenomena. All the organs of the body should have their chronicles, but it will be found that they are the wheels and springs of the time-piece. The chief index is remarked in the organs of mastication, and they respond to epochs. *

The young of all animals, whose early life depends upon maternal milk, must be endowed with a perfect and an acute sense of hearing. in order that the maternal call may be recognized, whether it be expressed by the coaxing, soothing tones of a fond woman over her helpless one, or the bleating, whining, moaning, or crying, of the lower animals. Hence, we find an amazing contrast here to the tardy development of teeth. The only portion of the skeleton, or bony fabric of mammals, which is found to be perfectly formed at birth, is the small bones of the ear, doubtless a wise provision for the conveyance of sound to the infant mind. The nursling is well acquainted with maternal language long before it can lisp its first tiny word, " Ma ;" just as every suckling in a flock recognizes its kindred " Baa," when it has strayed away, and gone beyond parental care and protection.

* "On Dentition." *J. Ashburner, M.D.*

C

A child becomes a fit subject for education from 2 to 3 years of age. An infant-school, when rightly constituted, is only a nursery on a large scale, where children can be reared in purer air, and better regulated circumstances, than when exposed to the sickening atmosphere of a small room, where the whole family both eat, drink, and sleep, or to the contaminating influences of street society. A piece of play-ground, flower borders and beds, circular swings, wooden prisms, of the form of bricks, for the purpose of building houses, towers, and other fanciful structures, map and picture puzzles, and such like amusements, should constitute the essential features of an infant-school. But, in this remark, too great stress cannot be laid on the character of the atmosphere of a public school. Amongst these establishments it is a common practice to keep the dormitories shut up. If you gaze on the faces of a group of children outside a schoolroom, you may readily discover, by the wan and sickly hue, those who have just left an apartment in which they have been respiring a deteriorated atmosphere, and those who have been playing in the open ground during the previous hour. Cleanliness of skin, also, among children, is almost as essential to health, as is the purity of the air they respire. The filthily dirty are proverbially the viciously immoral poor, and it has been well observed, that " if there be a lovely object to the human eye, it is a clean, clear-faced, healthy, innocent, neatly-clad, happy child." Parents who are utterly negligent of this paramount duty to their offspring, not only inflict an evil on the child, but diminish the esteem of those around them. A mother should accustom her child to the use of cold water as soon as the early stages of dentition are gone by. In order to do this effectually, presuming the child is born of healthy parents, and exhibits no signs of sickliness, the hot summer mornings should be taken advantage of, and cold washing adopted through the autumn, and, in some instances, children enjoy cold sponging through the greater part of winter.

FIRST STAGE.

INFANCY TO CHILDHOOD.

ONE TO SEVEN YEARS.

CHAPTER IV.

Infantile Mortality: its Three Main Causes, Domestic Duties in its Prevention, Maternal Ignorance in its Increase—" Dandriff," " Suck Thumb,"
" Cold in Head," &c., in Dentition.

WE need only take a cursory glance at those valuable records of
the Registrar-General, in order to satisfy our minds that infancy, to
twice seven years, embraces the most perilous epoch in the life of
man.   Thus, out of 1,508 deaths in one week in this metropolis,
682 occurred to children under 15; whilst only 501 belonged to
persons from 15 to 60 years; and 293 from 60 upwards, and this
is rather below the ordinary death-rate in the young.   The pre-
ponderance of sickness is from infancy to 3 and 4 years of age;
in other words, the whole period of dentition exposes the life of the
child to numerous mortal derangements.   I have now before me a
record of 249 cases of sickness which have come under my care at
the Western General Dispensary within the last six months; and,
out of this number, 69 were under 5 years of age, 35 of this
number were at or under 2 years, or rather more than 1-7th of
the whole.   My colleague, Dr. Merriman, has kindly furnished me
with his own experience.   In three years, at the same institution,

c 2

amongst 877 women and children, 526 were under 5 years of
age, 65 above that age, and the remainder (286) were women;
thus, we observe, that the great death-rate ranges from the period
of birth to 5 years of age, and then gradually declines.

What is the cause of this great amount of sickness amongst
children in London, as we know that it bears no resemblance to
the sick list of the country? The reply is very simple. Freshness
of air, wholesomeness of food, and cleanliness of body, are wholly
denied the bulk of the infantile poor of our wealthiest parishes
in the metropolis; and these form three mighty antidotes to many
diseases of childhood.

A deprivation of the first antidote, swells the death-list under
the heading of "Diseases of the Lungs," &c. Absence of the
second, gives us a large number of deaths under "Convulsions;"
whilst a want of cleanliness in person, in clothing, and in the home,
helps forward other calamities in a woeful degree, of which bowel
disorders, especially infantile cholera, are the most formidable.

The first death-cause may be obviated by very simple means.
As soon as the bed-room is vacated, the air should be changed in
summer by a free current from windows to door, and in winter by
a fire, with the door open. No offensive smells should pollute the
house under any circumstances, otherwise it must be no matter of
surprise if sore throat, loss of energy, and of appetite ensue.
Scarlet fever, diphtheria, or croup, may show itself. Yet, though
bad air kills its thousands of children indirectly, unwholesome food
kills its tens of thousands in an unmistakeable manner. Rickets,
Scrofula, Consumption, worms, and emaciation, are a few of the
maladies induced by this evil. Some time since, a medical friend
requested me to see an infant, fifteen months old, who was reduced
to a mere skeleton. Consumption existed on the maternal side,
but the children were pretty healthy. The patient had been weaned,
and the never-failing remedy of "tops and bottoms," "arrowroot,"
and bread-and-milk were resorted to; all but the last were absolutely pernicious, and even London milk cannot be called generous
and wholesome at all times. Fresh whey, pure corn flour, good

beef tea, genuine milk biscuits, cod liver oil (medicated), were amongst the chief articles prescribed, and in three months the child became plump and vigorous. It often happens, that where the family have a slight taint of Scrofula or of Consumption, the digestion is weak; and the greatest care is required in the management of the diet, lest bowel disorders should come on. A sister of the above infant, of three years of age, has recently suffered from periodical attacks of extreme pain in the stomach. The time at which the attacks came on pointed to the fact that they were connected with the passage of some crude, undigested matters, attempting to go through that wonderful piece of mechanism, the valve of the larger intestine; this faithful sentinel forbids the egress of any irritating substances, and spasmodically closes its portal against them—pain and distress follow. Drastic purgatives in the above case were injudiciously given, and relief obtained; but, alas! it was at the expense of weakening the membrane of the canal still farther, and thus the attacks became more frequent and more severe. It was ascertained that the child had been occasionally indulged with red or black currant jam, on bread, in order to keep up a lax habit of body, so as to avoid the farther use of aperients; but this plan brought on the attacks, in consequence of the crude seeds coming in contact with the irritable membrane of the valve, and thereby inducing pain. Meat, chopped, with or without potatoes, produced the same effect; and therefore the mother was strictly enjoined not to attempt to feed the child on any solid food for one month. Beef-tea, soups, light and thin puddings, thick milk, and honey on unfermented bread, were to form the usual diet, with some tonic medicines. The child is now rapidly gaining flesh, and has had no return of the seizures. In such cases of feeble digestion, with a pale skin and imperfectly nourished limbs, it is very desirable to accustom the child to cold sea-bathing, or some artificial substitute of that kind.

Dandriff, in children, is the plague of the nursery, the opprobrium of mothers, and the enemy of soap and water. Frequent and regular ablution of the forehead, where it first appears, rubbing the head dry, and applying some specific lotion, is desirable. The use of oil, grease, &c., is often more prejudicial than useful; for, in many cases of dentition, the secretion of greasy matter about the head and face is abundant. The increase of saliva, also, at this period, is very marked; so that not only do infants slobber very much before dentition, but the "suck thumb" habit appears to owe its origin to the relief which a constant flow of saliva affords to the turgid gums. Many observing mothers must have noticed that the cutting of every tooth is preceded by a regular sneezing and cold in the head, and during this period the bowels are torpid, and the infant feverish and out of sorts. Whenever this state of things comes on, the child should be put on spoon food exclusively.

SECOND STAGE.

CHILDHOOD TO YOUTH.

SEVEN TO FOURTEEN YEARS.

CHAPTER V.

Human Parasites; their symptoms and their domicile — Ringworm—
"Scald" Head—Squinting—Headache—Giddiness.

WATER, that essential element in animal and vegetable life, consists
of hydrogen and oxygen, chemically combined in a definite proportion. Of these two agents consist all kinds of water, and whatever matters are contained in them beside, they have nothing to do
with their composition, and are really extraneous. Therefore, when
vegetable productions abound in water, they indicate a positive
degree of impurity; but when animalculæ abound, a still higher
degree of impurity exists. Well-water may be charged with
mineral salts, and thus prove an irritant to the delicate stomach of
a child; whilst river, or surface water, may hold organic matters in
solution. Cold boiled water is the safest form to use under such
circumstances. There is a vulgar error abroad, that everything we
eat or drink teems with life, and that even our bodies abound with
minute living parasites. The notion is as disgusting as it is
erroneous.

Unwholesome water will produce weakness of digestion in the
young, and imprudent mothers are induced to allow them any food
they ask for, under the fallacious argument that "the poor little

thing has such a wretched appetite, that one is glad to give it any-thing it will eat."

The most singular nervous symptoms are often produced in children by the presence of worms. I have elsewhere related* a curious instance of this kind of cause and effect. A young girl was sent up from the country, with a long-standing cough of a most obstinate nature. It was deemed proper to keep her in the hospital for a week or so, in order to watch her case. She soon became feverish and generally disordered, owing to the change of residence. A brisk emetic was given her, followed by an aperient, under the expectation of cutting short this slight attack. They relieved her of an Entozoa, so common in this country—the " Tænia solium "—when fever and cough entirely subsided.

Cold salt sponging is of inestimable service in preventing such annoyances, for in health, with cleanliness, not a single organic production or animalcule of any description is present, either outwardly on the surface, or inwardly in the cavities of our bodies. It is only when the system becomes disordered, and cleanliness is not observed, that parasitical productions may be expected to spring up.

The singular co-existence of ring-worm with squinting, from the use of impure water, has been already pointed out in a record of one hundred and twenty cases of disorder in women † and children. A nervous squint and blindness are somewhat remarkable, and I cannot refrain from quoting one of the many singular cases recorded in that pamphlet.

" A woman was seized with giddiness, headache, loss of appetite, palpitation, alternate flushings, and clammy perspirations; and her son, eleven years old, was attacked with weight over the forehead, squinting, and, at length, blindness. They both partook of the well-water and canal-water of the Wolverton station, mixed; the former contained a large quantity of alkaline earths, and the last an unusual amount of organic substance, no doubt derived from the surface drainage of

---

* " Physiognomy of Diseases." By George Corfe, M.D.
† " Observations on the Effects of the Wolverton Waters, &c., as supplied to the Inhabitants."—*Pharmaceutical Journal,* 1848.

lands more or less covered with animal manure. As both mother and son had been under medical treatment at Wolverton without avail, and observing the equivocal nature of nervous symptoms in many of these people, I was led to conclude that the squint and headache arose from mere distress of, and not disease in, the brain. The son was ordered anthelmintic medicines, and his sight returned, the squinting diminished, his health improved, but it was co-existent with the riddance of a Tænia (tape-worm)."

Another troublesome parasite is to be met with on the surface of the body. That pest of schools, "scald-head," is a vegetable fungus, and bears a resemblance to the minute confervoid growths of the yeast plant, or mouldy substances in decayed animal matter. The "Blue Coat" School children were formerly notorious for its possession, and more than one-third of the boys were, usually at a distance from London, affected with the complaint. The medical officers revised the dietary role, and introduced a larger proportion of vegetables and of meat, whilst they diminished the amount of puddings and farinaceous food; since which time the disease is scarcely known amongst them.

One of the earliest symptoms which a child tainted with Scrofula may exhibit, either at the weaning period, or soon afterwards, is a weakness in the vessels of the eye. They weep, and the tears falling over the cheeks so influence the latter, that sores appear in various parts; by-and-by, intolerance of light supervenes, or rather the eyelids are spasmodically closed, and no effort on our part can open them, neither will the child suffer you to touch them. Not long since, the child of a medical friend was brought from the country to see me. As soon as he entered the room, with a bright sunlight shining on him, he skulked away into the darkest corner, putting on that singular grin which is so characteristic of the disease, and which is partly a frown, with the mouth half open, as if yawning. A worse case of scrofulous ophthalmia was never seen; and yet, in six weeks, the child became quite well, through a rigid attention to diet, change of air, and remedial measures of the most simple nature.

SECOND STAGE.

CHILDHOOD TO YOUTH.

SEVEN TO FOURTEEN YEARS.

CHAPTER VI.

Rickety Limbs—Consumption and Scrofula, their Causes and desolating Effects—Harrowing Scenes amongst the Poor—Benevolence in Food, &c.

PERSONS who visit this vast metropolis, and saunter through our parks, the " Lungs of London," at an hour when the middle classes send forth their little ones to get some fresh air, must have observed the numerous bandy-legged, bow-limbed, sallow-faced children in every direction, some cramped by iron boots, others with wooden splints bandaged around their legs. It is a piteous sight, and makes one's heart ache, because the most skilful man is utterly baffled in affording any relief to such cases. Yet preventive means may ward off evils which medical agents cannot cure. Rickets is a twin sister to scrofula. If you could obtain an hour's conversation with that very important and intelligent officer—" The Physician in Ordinary to the inhabitants of the Zoological Gardens in Regent's Park"—he would inform you that the monkeys are especially the subjects of scrofula, and that the beasts, as well as birds, brought over from warm climates, perish in great numbers from the same disease. The cause of this mortality does not arise from the impurity of the air, so much as from the excess of moisture succeeded by cold ; for, in proportion as the mean temperature of the day and night falls below $50\frac{1}{2}°$, human mortality (in the London districts at least) increases, and the same law presides over the brute creation. The practical lesson given to us by Dr. Farr * is the following :—Cold destroys a certain number of persons rapidly, and, in others, occasions diseases which prove fatal in four or five weeks. A great number of the aged, and of those afflicted with difficulty of breathing, cannot resist cold sunk so low as 32°. The temperature of the atmosphere in which they sleep can never safely descend lower than 40°, for if the cold that freezes water in their chamber does not freeze their blood, it impedes respiration ; and life ceases when the blood heat has sunk a few degrees below the standard of 98°. The prejudicial effect of impurity of air is more manifest on the constitution and future growth of the young during the first stage of life's seven years than upon any successive period. We find it stated † that in cities, as contrasted with rural districts, the deaths from con-sumption are increased 24 per cent. ; those from typhus, 55 per cent. ; and those from child-birth, 59 per cent. The diseases chiefly incidental to childhood are twice as fatal in the town districts as they are in the country. One striking fact is obtained from this Report, ·namely, that children under two years of age, although they get as much exercise as their tender age would allow of any-where, die in much larger numbers in town than in the country. Yet we do not wish to be misunderstood in this important matter. When scientific men speak of impure air, it is not implied that the atmosphere contains any specific poison of fever, ague, or small-pox, &c., &c., but, that impurity of the atmosphere excites the human frame to a predisposition to take up such poisons much sooner. There is no question but that scrofula is the direct result of impure air, and, when once established in the constitution, it passes down for several generations, an hereditary taint in the system. An

* The Registrar-General.
† Registrar-General's Annual Report.

exposure to cold and damp, with dormitories on the basement, adjoining a back yard, ten or twelve feet square, with open lattrines, are fruitful sources of it, and of diphtheria, fever, diarrhœa, and lung-diseases, with which this and other large cities abound.

Rickets, scrofula, and atrophy, usually manifest themselves at a period between nine months and two or three years old—that is, during the time of teething. The first evidences are a loose, flabby state of the skin and muscles; the limbs waste, whilst the joints become enlarged, and the vessels of the neck are distended, and the whole head increases in size.

Although it is not intended to introduce any specific line of treatment for such formidable diseases of infancy as the above, or scarlet fever, measles, small-pox, croup, &c., but only to confine these remarks to disorders of a lesser kind, yet a few hints may be added on the means necessary to be adopted for the mitigation of consumption and scrofula, &c.

Lord Ashburton once asked, " Why is it that one family can live in abundance where another starves? Why, in similar dwellings, are the children of one parent healthy, of the other, puny and ailing?" " It is not," he answers, " luck or chance that decides these differences; it is the patient observation of nature, which has suggested to some gifted minds rules for their guidance, which have escaped the heedlessness of others.

" We see a worthy couple doing their best to rear a young family to maturity. They rejoice in the smiles of the children, and their house is full of young life and its hopes. But one after another of the young people, as they reach a certain age, manifest a tendency to decline. It is found that a physical disease, with which the mother is partially affected, and which is known to have made great ravages in her family, is now beginning to show itself in the constitutions of those once hopeful children. The eldest born sinks, and has his share of bewailment. Another, if possible, more loved and more grieved over, follows. In short, one after another, this family fades away, leaving the parents at the last utterly desolate. Nothing can be more affecting than this, nothing can make a greater

demand upon the sympathy of friendly neighbours. We feel bound
to offer every suggestion of religious consolation to the hapless
pair. It seems cruel to hint, in the faintest manner, that they have
been, in any degree, the cause of drawing such a heart-break upon
themselves; and yet, when we take an extended view of the case,
we can be at no loss to see, that, with judicious forethought, the
calamity might have been prevented." Such is the truthful picture
drawn by a modern writer of the devastating ravages of consumption. But no persons can judge of the harrowing sights that are
daily met with by every medical practitioner in this huge metropolis; "thousands of the poor, not artizans, not labourers (for they
are comparatively an aristocracy), but street touters, fruit-sellers, and
others, who supply articles to those who need them, bivouac,
rather than lodge, in wretched half-furnished or unfurnished rooms,
half starving upon miserably small gains, and often without a means
of livelihood. It is the extremest picture of poverty, far beyond
anything that was ever presented in the northern land, once considered so beggarly, throwing into the shade any kind of misery
that ever occurs amongst the North American Indians." Let me
quote two instances deduced from this day's labour in the Lisson
Grove District, where my duties are assigned. In a low, dirty street,
resides a hatter, who ushered me down into his back kitchen (properly speaking, a back cellar), where I found a poor female lodger
lying on the ground, with a few rags over her, without bedstead,
giving forth that raven-like noise in respiration, so thoroughly
characteristic of acute suffering in the wind-pipe. In short, it was
active inflammation of the organ of voice, and, as she vainly struggled
to give me some idea of the suffocating attacks of breathlessness and
of impending death, that she had endured for twenty-four hours,
the poor creature became quite exhausted, and fell back on her
pillow of old coats, gowns, and other rags. The only person in the
room to wait on her was a girl, her daughter, about eight years old.
The husband is a street knife-grinder, and was out for the day's
work. The residence was just ten feet by eight, dark, and looking
into a filthy back yard, and the patient's head was close to the door,

an east wind had set in, and a hopelessness of doing any good
paralyzed one's efforts. She was urged to go to an adjoining
hospital, but declined the offer; so that, in such a place, with such
air and wretchedness, death may have released her ere this time.

The second case was that of an Irish fruit-hawker, in the last stage
of consumption. The room which he occupied was small, destitute of
every kind of comfort, excepting the bed on which he lay, the clothes
of which consisted of a tattered counterpane, covering old gowns,
&c., &c.; the house was overrun with dirty children, and the fetid
smells so overpowering, from filthy accumulations within and without, that, much as we are accustomed to have our olfactory nerves
assailed, the exhalations surpassed anything that I had previously
met with. At an old table sat two unfortunate girls, not related to
the man, devouring a plate full of hot steaks and bread, the wages
of sin, and who, for a small pittance, are allowed to bivouac in
this room, to cook and eat their food, &c. The wife of the patient
goes out "charring" by day, and leaves the nursing duties to the
casual visits of a neighbour. It may seem incredible to many, but
this poor ignorant man voluntarily quitted the workhouse hospital
for such a home, "rather than be starved to death in the union,"
as they asserted; whereas, in this parish, I can testify that the
medical attendance, comforts of bed and bedding, dietary scale,
nursing, and general management of the sick poor, are not equalled
by many unions, and certainly are surpassed by none. The wife
held three letters of admission into different hospitals given to her
by some benevolent persons, but they both declined to use them,
choosing rather such a home than all the charitable luxuries of a
well-regulated hospital or union. " Il n'y a qu'un pas entre le
sublime et le ridicule," was a remark of the First Napoleon. On
getting into the street, other objects of miserable poverty were
seen, a squalid woman with the loss of one eye, half-clad in tattered
rags, holding a baby, with an urchin at her side, was screaming
certain lines, that memorialized the solemn events connected with
the present season, in short, a Christmas carol, to the hackneyed
tune of " I'd choose to be a daisy." A kind helping hand to such

cases has been stretched out by many persons in this neighbourhood ; the clergy are indefatigable in their praiseworthy endeavours to alleivate human want; and amongst other excellent means of relief, ranks a "Soup kitchen," and an "Invalid's dinner-table." *

It is of the deepest importance to every parent that the exciting cause of any of these desolating evils should be traced out. Next to hereditary tendency, which may be so weak, that care and a favourable combination of circumstances might prevent the offspring from a manifestation of the disease, we have to consider other agents that exercise a power of developing consumption. Improper diet, which always implies imperfect nourishment, is one exciting cause. Mild and dry weather seldom promote either of these diseases. On the Continent, consumption is known under the title of the "English Disease," and certainly there is no climate where it sweeps off its hundreds and thousands as it does in our own islands. Infants at the breast, with abundance of good milk, seldom show any evidences of consumption or of scrofula ; whereas, as soon as they are weaned, they betray unequivocal signs of derangement in their digestive organs, unless an entire change is made in the whole *régime* of the family, and, sooner or later, the sufferers fall early victims to undeveloped scrofula or tubercular disease, known as consumption.

* This last was established, is managed, and admirably superintended, by the personal exertions of a benevolent lady, Miss Mayo, Hamilton Terrace, St. John's Wood.

THIRD STAGE.

YOUTH TO YOUNG MEN.

FOURTEEN TO TWENTY-ONE YEARS.

CHAPTER VII.

Malting—Brewing—Spirits and Fats—Cod Liver Oil—Is Consumption
curable?—Early Care and Management of delicate Children prone to it
—The deceitfulness of the Disease—Treachery of a Stomach Cough.

THE brewing of fermented liquors has become a trade of such considerable importance in this country, that it would require a princely
fortune to purchase even the utensils of one colossal establishment, and
it is, therefore, matter of the utmost importance that the conductors
of such firms should be acquainted with the principles of the materials which they employ, and with the nature of those changes
which take place during the course of fermentation.

The first great process is the conversion of starch in the barley
into sugar, and this change is effected in malting, for, during the
germination of plants (and malting is an imitation of this act), sugar
is formed out of the starch that surrounds the embryo of the seed.
Sugar is as necessary for young plants as it is for young children,
and the stomach of the latter must convert starchy food into sugar,
just as the vital power in the germinating embryo of the seed produces sugar out of the surrounding starch.

The analogy between a barley-corn and a birds' egg is greater than their dissimilarity in appearance would lead one to expect. The former is covered with its testaceous outside or husk, beneath which is the delicate membrane (spermo-derm) enclosing the tiny storehouse of food (starch) for the future plant; and inside the whole lies the "heart," or embryo, the undeveloped plant in miniature.

In the egg, there is beneath its shell a transparent membrane, enclosing the food (the albumen, or white) for the unhatched bird, and the yolk, in which lies the "cicatricula," or future chick. How long vitality may remain in each of these curious bodies unimpaired, is a question not yet settled. The statements relative to the germination of wheat found in mummies requires confirmation, though Professor Lindley mentions an instance of the growth of young plants from seeds found in an ancient barrow in Devonshire along with some coins of the Emperor Hadrian. But one mighty agent must appear on the *rôle* of life, ere re-production of species can take place in either case—this agent is heat; solar or artificial heat is as requisite for germination as natural heat is for incubation; though, in Egypt, artificial hatching is carried on to a great extent, in imitation of the natural instinct of the ostrich, "which leaveth her eggs in the earth, and warmeth them in the dust" (Job xxxix. 14).

Solar heat starts the embryo of barley into dependent existence; that is to say, the future blade struggles upwards to air, and the little root downwards to earth, both living on this starchy food, now converted by heat into sugar; and just when its first blade appears above ground to breathe vital air, we find its magazine of food below is exhausted.

In the egg, however, the little chick-life starts into being when "sitting" begins; and the temperature of the hen's breast is always raised a few degrees during this period.

The future bird finds its food ready to hand in the white of the egg, albumen being the most nutritive substance known by chemists; and it is not until the chick has consumed all its stored-up food, that it breaks its house of lime, and comes forth to live on air and on earth; in short, a breathing animal, whose wants are sup-

plied by the fruits, &c., of the ground. Wonderful contrivance!
Inscrutable Wisdom and Design! Thus—

"Leaves, lungs, and gills, the vital ether breathe,
On earth's green surface, or the waves beneath."

Now, the sugar alluded to in speaking of malt is wholly different
from that we consume at our tea-table. We have the sugar of the
cane plant, known as cane sugar, and that of sweet fruits and
vegetables, usually called grape sugar. The first is crystallizable,
but incapable of true fermentation, and, therefore, alcohol is not
extracted from it ; the latter is the source of our various spirits from
grain, as gin, brandy, whisky, &c.; and thus we may paraphrase
Darwin's lines on the " Will-o'-Wisp," and say of the spirit lamp—

"Thus heat imparted to some cereal grains,
Expands the kindling atoms into flames."

This sugar abounds in honey, also sugar is abundant in the milk
of all mammalia, and may be given to children with impunity, nay,
it is advantageous in proper quantities; but the obese, gouty, or
dyspeptic parents must avoid it, although a teetotaller may use it ;
whilst a spirit-drinker swallows it under another form.

The earliest indication of a weak or impaired digestion in a child
is manifested in its inability to convert starchy matters into sugar.
The stomach often turns against the latter article of food, from an
intuitive disrelish of it under an artificial form, though sugar is
more easily taken up and more available than starch ; starch and
sugar contain nearly half their weight of carbon (charcoal principle),
whilst fats, oil, and butter, contain 4-5ths of carbon. This car-
bonaceous matter is the fuel for the maintenance of animal heat, or
combustion ; and the greater the amount of carbon in the food, the
better is maintained the temperature of the body, independent of its
promoting the nourishment of the various parts. This is the simple
explanation of the beneficial effects of cod liver oil in consumption,
and of its injury in corpulent, bilious constitutions. As animal fat
or starchy food (farina), enter so largely into the nutrient materials
for the young, it may be interesting to observe the relative composition of these four agents.

	Carbon.	Hydrogen.	Oxygen.
Starch consists of	24	20	20
Sugar ,, ...	24	28	28
Alcohol ,, ...	16	24	8
Fat ,, ...	66	10	8

The celebrated chemist, Leibig, describes the change which each undergoes in the animal body, thus :—The hydrogen is oxidized, and water is formed, whilst the remaining oxygen with carbon forms carbonic acid, which is expired from the lungs and skin; so that " no true combustion of carbon occurs in the living body, but the carbonic acid is formed by a process of substitution in this case, and exhaled." It has been already hinted that some stomachs cannot digest fatty matters. The organ rebels at it, struggles to get rid of it, and that nauseous taste in the throat, known as " heartburn," or biliousness, supervenes, with disagreeable feelings in the head, dreams, and lethargy of mind and body. This is one of the ordinary results of an indulgence in fat, greasy foods. The cure is very simple, when the cause is known ; but as long as people think it is bile, they will have recourse to all kinds of " antibilious pills," and the results are, " an injured stomach, impure blood, serious disease, and not unfrequently an untimely grave." The epitaph on the unfortunate gentleman's tomb at Rome, who, it is said, took medicine when well, and soon became ill, may be inscribed over such a grave :—

> "I once was well,
> I would be better:
> I took physic,
> And here I am."

Let us now inquire—is consumption curable when manifested. or capable of being prevented in manifesting itself *when dormant?* The very term consumption implies that the disease is wasting, and, therefore, it is only applicable to the development of the complaint in all its peculiar symptoms. Employing the word, therefore, in this sense, we may readily give an answer to the first part of the inquiry, and observe that well-authenticated cases are on record, and some have come under the author's notice, in which unequivocal consumption was cured, and the subjects of it are now alive, and in excellent health.

With respect to the latter part of the question, whether it may be prevented in its outbreak, there can be little doubt, with the vast information we have lately obtained from a knowledge of Hygeinic rules, sanitary laws, and the *modus operandi* of certain valuable agents in medicine, with outward appliances—as respirators, counter-irritants, &c., &c.—that this devastating malady of Great Britain may be arrested, if not finally cured, in those who are prone to it, by judicious and patient medical treatment in its early stages. Dr. Passavoine tells us, that amongst 920 children, 3-5ths of the whole, or 538, died from this disease, between two to fifteen years of age. One of the principal objects to be gained in the prevention of the development of the disease in a delicate child is, to insure wholesome air in the sleeping apartment, not to suffer the patient to share the bed with another child, to ascertain that its residence is on a dry soil, and well drained, in a mild and equable climate. Exercise should be moderate, the hours of rising and rest punctual and early, the clothing warm, but always suitable to the season ; the food must be nourishing, without stimulants ; the skin kept clean, and those myriads of cutaneous lungs known as pores,* are to be maintained free and open by means of frequent tepid ablution in winter, and by cold bathing in summer. Moderate study should be insisted on, and exhausting indulgences of all kinds absolutely forbidden. Not less important is the time at which a child with a consumptive or scrofulous tendency should be within doors. From sunrise to sunset during the six winter months, and from eight to eight in the height of summer, may be regarded as the safest rule for out-door recreation ; but in the depth of winter, the restriction must be even greater, and from ten or eleven to three only the child should be allowed to be in the air ; and when at home, the nursery, in which a fire must be kept, should be at the top, rather than at the bottom of the house.

Consumption, at a very early period of life, differs in its symptoms

* Embracing fifty-two miles of surface !

from the same disease in full-grown persons. The cough is more deceitful in its nature, and when it follows whooping-cough, it is too often supposed to be only the sequelæ of the latter complaint, whereas the wasting malady is slowly and silently doing its work of destruction. The attacks of cough in this form of infantile consumption often seize the little patient in paroxysms, with no expectoration, and but little fever. The glands in the neck and throat may be observed to enlarge, the appetite becomes capricious, and, after an ordinary meal of solid food, this spasmodic kind of cough will set in, until the whole meal is brought up, and the child, exhausted, lies down, and falls off into a doze.

THIRD STAGE.

YOUTH TO YOUNG MEN.

FOURTEEN TO TWENTY-ONE YEARS.

CHAPTER VIII.

Second Dentition; its Irregularities and Disorders—Headache and Epilepsy (?)—St. Vitus-dance—Hysteria; Nervous Children and their Bad
Habits.

A POPULAR preacher once stated that he never knew what it was
to dream; most probably, therefore, he never suffered from headache, for those who are distressed with the one, usually know something of the other. Yet the causes of headache are as obscure, in
many instances, as the origin of dreams.

A lady consulted me lately on a species of headache to which her
eldest daughter, of fourteen, was continually subject; it began over
one brow, after much reading or study, moved down the face, and
fixed itself in the jaws. There was a wan, saddened cast in the
features; and on inspection of the teeth, there appeared two or three
unable to get through from simple crowding of the fangs, or consequent overlapping of the crowns together. The patient was listless,
and would take no exercise, so that she was indulged with lying on
the sofa the greater part of the day. Some teeth were extracted:
the headaches subsided, and the general health shortly improved.
It is in this second dentition as well as in the first teething that we

find so many and such alarming nervous symptoms spring up during its progress; and the fact that no pain exists in the teeth themselves, or in the jaw, naturally misleads many anxious parents from the true source of the malady, until the nervous irritation has gone on unmitigated, to the production of an epileptic seizure or a fit of convulsions.* The following case, under my own notice, is a fair specimen of numerous instances of the same kind. A lad, aged fifteen, from the plough-tail, was affected with epileptic fits; he had suffered from them several years, and had derived no benefit from the medical treatment pursued in the country. He was six weeks under the use of remedies usually resorted to in such cases, but finding no good results follow, he was requested to lose several badly decayed double teeth, though he had not experienced the least inconvenience from them : however, on removal of these, the fangs were found much diseased and enlarged, and although he had suffered from two or three fits a day, yet, eighteen months subsequent to their extraction, not one fit had recurred. There can be no doubt, therefore, of the intimate union between cause and effect in this instance. But a far more instructive case than the preceding has just been under my care. A youth about eighteen years of age, by trade a carpenter, was seized with epilepsy whilst at the bench at work, in Berkshire. His father brought him to me under very singular circumstances, to which allusion shall be made in a future chapter. The lad presented the appearance of rude health, but the description given of the nature of the seizure, his own account of himself, and his general demeanour, convinced me that the derangement was *without* the brain (eccentric), rather than from disease

* " We are all so familiar with the occurrence of convulsions during the first dentition, that in infancy the risk is rather of the grave disease to which they are possibly due being overlooked, than of the influence of teething in their production being underrated. On the other hand, the occasional share of the second dentition in exciting epileptic or other convulsive seizures is too little borne in mind, and a graver prognosis than the event justifies is sometimes expressed in consequence."—*West's Lectures.*

within the nervous matter (centric). Various remedies were tried, though without much hope of his becoming benefited thereby ; for on looking into his mouth, the molar teeth were so dangerously crowded, that on questioning him more closely, he acknowledged that his jaw ached dreadfully sometimes, especially after a meal, and this was frequently followed by headache. He was prevailed on to lose several double teeth, and more than a year has elapsed, and no fit has recurred. One of the most exciting causes of epilepsy in a child of a weak and nervous habit is fright, or strong mental emotion; but pain or disturbance of any of the principal functions of the body may excite the disease, and, like St. Vitus-dance, lead on to imbecility of mind.

This latter disease is usually the result of some irritation upon the nervous system along the course of the alimentary canal, or in the irregular development of the permanent teeth. The disposition to nervous disorders is of course stronger in females than in males, and in those having dark eyes and hair than in the fairer ones. It is most common amongst girls and boys from the eighth to the eighteenth year, or that period included between the second dentition and puberty; and it is frequently brought on by an indulgence in raw, unripe fruit, sweets, heavy dumplings, and such like unwholesome food. The same causes may lead to hysteria, in a constitution prone to be " nervous." The most serious mistakes are sometimes made in the recognition of this last derangement of the system ; the damage that accrues to the sufferer, and the discredit to the practitioner, are oftentimes irreparable. In children, spasmodic complaints like the above are also easily excited by improper diet; whilst in adult women there is always some specific constitutional derangement, which re-acts upon the mind, and produces the disorder.

A plump, well-formed child, ten years of age, in the hospital, was kept on her back for reputed spinal disease ; the countenance was placid, the voice unusually deep-toned, but the lower limbs were to all appearance utterly powerless. A physician and surgeon agreed that the complaint was purely nervous, and unconnected with any disease. Cold affusion to the body, a determination to coax or scold her into an attempt to try and move about, succeeded in a week or more in making her walk alone ; but having a great aversion to be made a spectacle of in a public ward, she was allowed to join arm in arm with a child suffering from St. Vitus-dance of the left side. The girl always took the right or steady arm of the latter patient, but when she was desired to take the other, she looked archly up in my face, and observed, " Oh, sir, that's the dance arm, and I can't hold by that." She was, however, ordered to make friends with the dance arm, and as the girl was half a foot taller than this child, her wriggling motions, as they walked side by side, soon brought the other to feel that walking *without* such a restless companion was far the more pleasant mode of progression. The most valuable agents in warding off this insidious complaint are the constant use of the shower, or Douche bath, exercise in the open air, light nourishing food, regular hours, and absence of all stimulants, whether mental or dietary.

Some children, especially boys, grow into a habit of frowning, sniffing, or even snorting in a kind of spasmodic fit, or they may contract an occasional nod of the head, twitch of the mouth, winking of the eyes, &c.; and these habits may become so confirmed, that it is an impossible task to break them off. The only effectual mode of curing such disagreeable and unsightly tricks (if severe and repeated scolding fails), is to resort to the daily use of a shower-bath, from the back of the head to the whole course of the spine.

Alterations of structure and development of organs exercise a reciprocal action on one another. Until an individual has completed the fourteenth year, the nervous system is specially engaged in developing the teeth, jaws, and other organs of alimentation. After this epoch, the reproductive organs are called into vigour and activity; and it has been well observed, that " fewer inconveniences attend on dentition, when the process goes on slowly, than when it is more rapid," whilst, if the teeth be not fully developed, there may be a retardation of growth in the organs of reproduction.*

* Dr. John Clarke's " Commentaries."

THIRD STAGE.

YOUTH TO YOUNG MEN.

FOURTEEN TO TWENTY-ONE YEARS.

CHAPTER IX.

Boils and Blains—Poverty of Blood—Feeble Constitutions—" Green " Sickness—Hysteria—Noises in the Head—Victims of Homœopathy.

THE first appearance in Europe of that formidable scourge, Asiatic cholera, was about 1832-33 ; and since that period, boils or pustules, known as blains, have been more prevalent than in the earlier part of this century. We do not attribute any connexion to the two diseases, beyond the fact that the former scourge left traces of its having depreciated the bodily tone and vital energy of all classes of society, so that acute diseases cannot be met by such active remedies as we know they were accustomed to receive in the periods antecedent to the visitation of cholera in these islands.

These boils, &c., will run their troublesome course, and scarcely yield to any change of food. It is essential, however, that a patient should rigidly abstain from all sweets, and adopt a generous diet. There is no doubt that the same deranged condition of the system may lead to a scurvy state of the blood ; in other words, this life-maintaining fluid becomes thinner and more watery than in robust health ; its red or scarlet colour partakes more of a darkish blue, the mind grows indolent, and the functions of the body are disordered in consequence. Closely allied to this state of the blood is that condition we all know by the term " poverty of blood." In young women especially, the disorder first begins by an imperfect assimilation of food. Animal diet or flesh-forming material is disrelished ; pastry, hard dumplings, sweets, and preserves are greedily devoured ; and that faithful index of the state of the animal frame, the physiognomy, soon betrays the sickliness of the individual. The lips, and even tongue, at length become white; a waxy face, puffy eyelids and ankles, palpitation and breathlessness on the slightest exertion, gradually supervene ; and if a finger is cut, or the nose bleeds, the blood is so pale and thin, that it is commonly observed to be " turned into water." Now the blood is fed by the chyle, a fluid extracted from generous food ; and if this feeding of the life-giving circulation is arrested, checked, or altered, the constituents of the blood are reduced considerably below the standard of health. Depression of spirits, languor, and mental incapacity for ordinary study or work, succeed these changes ; and if there should unfortunately be a pre-disposition, by hereditary taint or otherwise, to consumption, scrofula, or such like diseases, the system will show a tendency to fall under the power of them. Hence cough, emaciation, and loss of strength come and go, hand in hand ; the parent apprehends it is only a cold or trifling disorder, administers some family medicine, with gruel, arrowroot, and such like spoon food, at bed-time, to encourage perspiration ; and thereby the blood is still further thinned, and the patient reduced to a weaker condition than before.

The disease popularly known as " green sickness," principally affecting young females, is likely to show itself under such circumstances as those now detailed. The face becomes yellowish-green, hence the origin of the name of the disease, which is further characterized by languor, palpitations, listlessness, pains in the back and loins, acidity on the stomach, and flatulence. The most depraved appetite often comes on, such as a craving for lime or chalk, and similar antacids ; all these symptoms indicate an utter loss of tone in the digestive powers, and if not early attended to, will pass on to a severer class of ailments, and the sufferer is apt to be affected with many of those insidious ailments known under the term hysterical. The judicious management of such cases in an early stage by a medical practitioner is of incalculable importance, and mothers should seek the benefit of it, rather than increase the malady by domestic nostrums, empirical medicines, improper diet, &c.

The habit of a female is much connected with the production of hysteria. Inactivity, grief, or anxiety of mind, with a sedentary life, and a constant use of a low diet, or of unwholesome, non-nutritious food, predisposes to this attack. Its disposition to pass into an epileptiform disease, renders its distinction from all other nervous affections of paramount importance. This disposition may be more easily prevented than cured ; " but upon this point medical men are not consulted. Parents do not foresee the misery they are often laying up for their daughters, by the unnatural mode of life to which they are subjected, for the sake of giving them fashionable accomplishments." *

It has been usual to ascribe to hysteria a variety of neuralgic affections to which young women are subject. Pain over one brow (brow ague) coming on at certain periods ; the stitch in the left side, occurring in girls whose habits are sedentary, or whose minds are easily disturbed by domestic anxieties ; flatulence, fulness in the throat, difficulty in swallowing ; such and other symptoms are usually placed to the account of hysterical affections. They occur most frequently in young women between sixteen and twenty-five, or later (according to Dr. Ashburner), if the wisdom teeth are not cut. The sufferers obtain but little sympathy from those around them, unless it spring from maternal or sisterly affection ; and then ofttimes, this sympathy is apt to lead the relatives into an undue regard of the ailments of the patient, and thus they foster rather than repress an unhealthy tone of mind. However, the malady is no less an evil and a distress ; and on that account it behoves us to watch carefully, and to attend sedulously to the early outbreak of such a disordered state of the nervous system, lest a more alarming

* Dr. Watson.

train of symptoms dawn upon us. At this moment a lady is under my care, who suffers from the most distressing attacks in her head; they commence at all hours of the day, and under all circumstances, by a gentle whizzing in the ears, which increases to a hissing, and at length to a roar, like a steam-engine ; at other times she is seized with a sudden feeling that the room, the house, and even the ground she stands on, are precipitously rushing forward, and carrying her, with indescribable velocity, in the moving mass. Her piteous cry, " Hold my head! Hold my head !" gives instant notice of the attack. The pulse rises to a feverish height, the face becomes pale, the hands and feet are stone cold, the heart throbs at a tumultuous rate, and the whole frame is shaken to its very centre ; so that hours elapse before the system is calmed into a natural condition. On a careful examination, there is no evidence whatever of actual disease ; but the unhealty state of the teeth and jaws, and the imperfect development of them, warrants one in asserting that the attacks owe their origin, in some measure, to an eccentric * irritation on the nerves of the head and face. Tonics, light and nutritious diet, cheerful society, and exercise daily in an open carriage, have so far relieved her, that she is now lively and active, and considers herself quite well. Such attacks, oft repeated, will usually lead on to great depression of spirits, grave forebodings of some calamity about to overtake the patient, and even a confirmed hypochondriacal state of mind. In these persons "there is a languor, listlessness, or want of resolution and activity with respect to all undertakings ; a disposition to seriousness, sadness, and timidity as to all future events ; an apprehension of the worst or most unhappy state of them ; and, therefore, often upon slight grounds, an apprehension of great evil."† This state of depression is often connected with disordered stomach, and that, too, of a most obstinate nature ; and nothing less than an entire revolution in the diet and general system of " tenir-mènage" will effectually eradicate this bias to hypochondriasis. It is in vain to pooh-pooh such per-

* Implying irritation *without,* and not *within,* the brain.
† Cullen's " Nosology."

sons with the usual charge of "You look very well," "You are only nervous; do stir yourself, and shake it off." The advice is either sneered at, or treated as the fruit of an unfeeling, ignorant mind. It is no wonder, therefore, if such individuals, whose cases are either misunderstood, or treated with contempt, call in the aid of empirics, Homœopaths, or resort to patent medicines and other nostrums. A clergyman's wife was under my care, some years ago, suffering with such attacks as those just described; she obtained great relief from an alterative line of treatment, and was apparently quite well for months, when some imprudence in diet brought back the attacks with increased severity, and for the relief of which she had recourse to calomel and other purgatives; this occurred at the period when Asiatic cholera was raging in England, and the relaxation suddenly took a form of choleraic diarrhœa, under which she gradually sank, with all the virulent symptoms of that frightful scourge.

FOURTH STAGE.

YOUNG MEN TO MEN.

, TWENTY-ONE TO TWENTY-EIGHT YEARS.

CHAPTER X.

Railway Travelling and its Evils—The Stomach, its Mazes and Mysteries
—Digestion and Indigestion—Meal-time and its Abuses.

IT is surprising how many aches and pains creep over us from
causes wholly under our control. In these days of rapid movement, from Ben Nevis to Land's-End, within as many hours as
would have occupied weeks in our childhood, there is not a more
fruitful cause of disturbance to the brain, and consequent headache,
than frequent or imprudent railway travelling. If my readers will
watch a passenger in a carriage, seated with his face to the engine,
eagerly looking out of the window of a "fast train" on approaching
objects, they will observe that the eye-balls oscillate rapidly, as
they momentarily glance at hills and dales, hedges and trees, gates
and meadows, rivers and roads. Then let them notice the eyes of
another individual seated with his back to the engine, and they will
see that the vision is only calmly employed in watching some distant
object as it gradually recedes in the distance.

The effect on the former person often induces headache or
sleepiness, if not a worse and more enduring evil. A city mer-
chant, through domestic affliction, was induced to break up his

London home and retire to Brighton, still visiting his counting-house daily by the " 9 a.m. express," and returning to dine at Brighton by the " 5 p.m. express." Matters went on satisfactorily for a few months, when he was conscious of some defect in his arithmetical powers ; he could not command his attention sufficiently to add up accounts, or transact other money matters ; in a few more weeks he found himself suffering daily from a sad frontal head-ache, which usually got worse before night ; and at length he sought medical advice for it. No relief was obtained by various kinds of treatment, and his physician urged him to remain one month at Brighton, without travelling, and omit all medicine. The effect was surprising ; he thoroughly lost his headache, and the former elasticity of his mind. returned, accompanied with great cheerfulness of spirits. Once more he ventured, morning and evening, by "the express ;" but former troubles returned with in-creased pain in the forehead, until he was so convinced that such imprudent travelling was detrimental to health, that he again broke up his home in Brighton, and returned to London. The above is but one of the many instances that might be adduced of the in-jurious effects of constant journeys by rail.

It was a favourite axiom with the celebrated French physician Chomel, that half the diseases of an Englishman arose from his indulgence in tea and beer. That " John Bull" is proverbially a gourmand, there can be do doubt ; but how far his manifold diseases are brought on by indulgence in the beverages referred to, is another question. It would be nearer the truth if we were to assert that three-fourths of the ailments of adults arise from abuse in eating and drinking, rather than from the improper quality of food. The stomach of a human being is that marvellous chemical laboratory in which every kind of material must be "got up" for the supply of the wants induced by the wear and tear of that mysterious struc-ture, with its millions of wheels within wheels, the living body. In one of the hidden, dark recesses of this vital alambic, matter must be extracted to build up or renew the brain and spinal cord, with their countless nerves ; in another corner, food must be concocted

for the ceaseless pumping work of that wondrous hydraulic machine, the heart, with its innumerable arteries, as well as for the
voluntary muscles of the body—450 and upwards in number. The
fingers that hold this pen, and the delicate eye that reads this line,
must be as carefully attended to, and their wants supplied, hour
by hour, as any other portion of the frame. But what can we
say of that mighty fabric, the skeleton, with its 254 bones? The
same fluid that supplies the eye with a tear, the mouth with saliva,
the liver with bile, or the skin with moisture, also " hedges up,"
moment by moment, the gradual decline of this osseous scaffolding,
of which Job thus speaks: "Thine hands have made me, * and
fashioned me together round about; Thou hast clothed me with
skin and flesh, and hast fenced † me with bones and sinews." An
animal world also in miniature is contained in the blood; and this
life-giving, life-maintaining fluid, is wholly derived from the quiet,
healthy, and regular elaborations of that chemical closet, the
stomach. There we find a substance which turns starch of rice,
potato, &c., into sugar; another to deprive meat of its fibrine; a
third to extract albumen from fish, or oil from fat; nay, it would
fill a volume to enlarge on the many operations of the stomach of
a healthy man. One of the earliest blows that my youthful scepti-
cism received came from a consideration of the impenetrable mystery hidden under the facts that the gland, secreting a tear, had
no power to secrete saliva; and that the liver could no more send
out perspiration in lieu of bile, than it could create itself. No!
Each organ has life in itself; and each, " after its kind," performs
that rôle in the human economy which the Divine hand of the Cre-
ator " took pains" to establish, when He made man after His own
image, and pronounced all His works " very good." Thus,

> " Organic forms with chemic changes strive,
> Live but to die, and die but to revive."‡

But the stomach may be styled the paragon of wonders within us;

---

* " Took pains about me."   † " Hedged."
‡ Darwin.

E

no sooner does it receive its quantum of matter, than (like a busy, clever, and indefatigable artificer), it immediately sets to work to dispose of the materials to the very best advantage, and with the least demand upon other neighbouring parts, although they *are* shortly called upon to aid this important organ. The food is first churned by a sort of revolving power, which the muscular bands of the stomach give to it; and this process serves to mix it thoroughly with that mighty solvent agent of the organ, gastric juice. As soon as this step is gained, the substance gradually divides itself into two distinct portions—the nutrient and the non-nutrient parts. The former is destined for the life-giving blood, the latter being the refuse. The whole operation varies from two to five hours, according to the quantity and quality of the food taken. It should be borne in mind, by every person who suffers from weak digestion, that this juice is constantly flowing into the stomach, though much less is present during the night than in the day; and if due attention is not given to this fact, so as to afford the juice employment, it will *do mischief;* in other words, if there is no food to dissolve, the coats of the stomach become still further enfeebled by the presence of this juice, which at length deteriorates from its original purity and activity. One of the main causes of disordered stomach, lowness of spirits, and enervation of mind, arises from a very prevalent fashion of huddling three meals into a few hours. Breakfast is taken at ten or eleven ; at two a hearty meal is made of meat, hashes, and vegetables—and this is termed a luncheon; at six, a dinner, with wine and coffee, completes the daily ration ; and thus the stomach is left fifteen or sixteen hours idle, whilst it has had to accomplish, in seven or eight, the work of eighteen hours. Three meals, at a distance of six hours from each, will always prove the standard by which a valetudinarian, from indigestion, may be guided. A few weeks ago, a gentleman from the country applied to me for advice under the following circumstances :—He stated that, although he led an active life in the open air, either by riding or walking—which, by-the-by, never exceeded two miles daily—yet he was troubled with increasing obesity, flatulence, palpitation, loss of sleep, great depression of spirits ; and this became so overpowering, that he was compelled to lie down sometimes two or four hours in the day. His age was thirty-six, and yet he looked forty-eight or fifty. Having listened to his tale of evils, and ascertained that he had no organic disease to account for such equivocal symptoms, I at once requested him to inform me how he lived. He stated that he usually breakfasted at seven or eight, and partook of a steak or mutton chop ; dined at one, on meat, vegetables, ale, pastry, &c. ; drank tea at six ; and supped at nine, on cold meat, with beer and grog; and yet, with all this amount of food, he was surprised to find himself growing weak, though fat. Here was an instance of a man giving the stomach as much animal food in one day as it should have had, under the circumstances, in three. Eight ounces of uncooked meat is an ample supply for one person daily ; whilst in this case at least three, and often four times that quantity was taken. He was desired to live on fish three days a week, meat once on the alternate days, and to take light claret and water in lieu of beer or grog. His exercise was to be on horseback only, and with some tonic alterative medicines, he was requested to give the plan one month's trial. It was upwards of three or more months ere he returned to inform me of his complete restoration, and he was especially pleased to find that he now knew not only what to eat ; but when, and how much to eat, a secret often learnt after the experience of long suffering.

FOURTH STAGE.

YOUNG MEN TO MEN.

TWENTY-ONE TO TWENTY-EIGHT YEARS.

CHAPTER XI.

The Stomach in Fish, Flesh, and Fowl—Vegetable Feeders and Flesh Eaters—Poison in a Tea-pot—Adulterated Food, and its pernicious Fruits.

THE mechanism, use, and vital importance of the digestive organ in man, cannot be better illustrated than by glancing at the development of that apparatus, from the lowest grade of animal life to that in the " lord of the creation." A stomach of some kind or other is to be met with in all animals, whether land or aquatic, otherwise nutrition and growth could not be maintained. The lowest type of stomach is seen in the sea anemone (*Cras*) : its several arms, mouths, or tentacula, not only seize the food, but convey it to a hollow pouch or stomach ; there its juices are abstracted, and the remainder is returned by the same route. The common leech is provided with a series of honeycomb-like cells throughout its whole body, and these may be styled its one stomach. Carnivorous beasts have only a bag as a stomach, and digestion with them is easy and rapid. Grass-feeders, on the other hand, have to digest a more tough and less organized substance than flesh-eaters ; and therefore they are endowed with three or more stomachs, into which the food passes in succession, " the cud chewed " always taking priority of passage to the unchewed meal.   Birds, on the other hand, have a species of mouth, with saliva, beyond the tongue and gullet, known as the crop or sap-bag, in which cavity the food undergoes a process of softening, very analogous to the act of human mastication; it is then introduced into the *true* stomach (the gizzard), where it is subjected to a most powerful trituration, by means of small pebbles, &c. Squeezed round and round by the action of its strong muscles, it is mixed with the gastric juice, and then emerges from the gizzard into the alimentary canal, to allow its nutrient portions to be sucked up by the innumerable ducts ready and waiting to convey them to the vital fluid—the blood.   The Crustaceans, as lobsters and crabs, have no need of pebble-stones, since their stomachs are provided with three or four teeth, which assist in grinding down the tough sea-weed on which they feed.   Each of the foregoing types of digestion has its representative in man, a consideration of which fact must convince every sensible mind that man is created an omnivorous being ; that is to say, his digestive organs evidence that he is intended to be a flesh and a vegetable feeder, and when he is deprived for any period of the former, and has to endure bodily labour and mental anxiety, the intense craving for meat of some form is so overpowering, that a civilized mind has not recoiled at the idea of cannibalism.   Dr. Livingstone describes his own feeling after being without animal food for a long period, under the trying climate of Africa ; and he speaks of it as an insupportable craving, so that when a buffalo was captured, the flesh was put warm on the fire, and eaten with the greatest avidity, before it was half-cooked.

This instinctive craving for animal sustenance by him who is to live by the sweat of his brow, evidences a law in our organization of great importance, namely, that the nutrition of our bodies is to be obtained from the animal as well as from the vegetable kingdom. We cannot thrive on purely vegetable, nor on purely animal food. There are principles in the latter which are essential to our very being, in health.   The animal kingdom is wholly supplied by the vegetable world ; and a purely carnivorous beast, as the lion, is indebted to this kingdom for support, as his prey is derived from vegetable feeders. Vegetation again is dependent on heat, rain, and soil, &c., &c.; and these agents are received from the clouds and the earth, hence the beauty and order of creation. Light was called into existence the first day; the Heavens, the second; the Earth, and its fruitful herb-bearing surface, the third day; whilst fowl, beast, and lastly, man, did not appear until the fifth and sixth day, or when, in fact, there was abundance of food for their support.

It has been already remarked, that more cases of indigestion arise from abuse in our daily food, than from the quality of the food eaten; and, doubtless, as a nation, we are excessive flesh, and scanty vegetable eaters, while our neighbours across the channel are the reverse in this matter. A very large class of kind, hospitable country friends, can scarcely recognize you as a real guest, if, when you pay them a visit, you do not eat and drink almost every hour in the day; and any excuse on your part to avoid running the gauntlet is construed into coldness, unfriendliness, and so forth; but the only rescue from such a martyrdom is to beat a retreat ere you are laid up with gout, bilious fever, or apoplexy, and part on amicable terms before any damage is done by such well-meant hospitality.

It is astonishing how long the human stomach will calmly submit to be bullied into a performance of work it was never destined to execute. Thus, if we give it a poison to dispose of, instead of resenting the injury, like a malicious person, it calmly strives to keep all quiet, and make the best of a bad business. Witness the amount of poison we put into this vital laboratory, month after month, and year by year, in the form of adulterated food; and do not let my country friends chuckle at the thought that all *they* eat and drink is wholesome and sound, because they " don't have it from London." Let us examine one article alone in the dietary scale that is purely English. Tea—who does not enjoy a good cup of Souchong or Congou ? What a soothing, cheering beverage is an infusion of Bohea? But mark the fact: we have all kinds of herbs passed upon us as tea, and if we examine one species of it—

green tea, for example—we shall find that fifteen cases in every twenty contain tea faced with prussian blue, or one of the bases of prussic acid. We are indebted to Mr. Warrington for this analysis, who states that the Chinese by such means can readily convert a green tea, withered and useless, into a black tea; or a "used up" black tea may be easily passed off as a green tea; but "such teas are never consumed in China, they are invariably exported, and, mainly, to these islands."*

It is a well-known fact, that blue is a favourite colour with the Chinese; and, fifty years ago, we exported to Canton annually 253,200 pounds of prussian blue. The trade is now virtually at an end. A common Chinese sailor came over in an East Indiaman, frequented a manufactory where the drug was prepared, learnt the art, returned to China, and there established a similar manufactory with such success, that the whole empire is now supplied with native prussian blue (ferro sesquicyanide of iron).†

As we have now arrived · at the period of life in which men and women are especially susceptible to disordered stomach and deranged nervous system from this kind of poison in tea, let me make a few remarks on a singular train of symptoms that come on in females chiefly (which, if not caused wholly by tea, are unquestionably aggravated by its use), but which are no where classified, as far as I can find, by medical authors, nor are they traced up to their true source, if noticed by any writer. The individuals who are most prone to the attacks now about to be described, are those who have endured great mental anxiety, and who inherit a gouty habit; who live freely on animal food, are variable in their flow of spirits, and are disposed to brood over present calamities, and forebode greater ones.

The symptoms are ofttimes ushered in with occasional flushings of the face, succeeded by more or less perspiration, a sense of faintness, and subsequent depression of spirits : sudden pain will ensue,

* " Pharmaceutical Journal," and "Davis's Chinese," vol. ii., p. 468.
† " Proceedings of the Chemical Society."—*M'Culloch's Dictionary*.

either over one temple, or at the top of the head, and sometimes at the back of it; the act of combing and brushing the hair painfully increases the ailment. As the disorder advances, noises in the head come on, such as humming, buzzing, singing, rumbling. One lady under my care always described the noise as that of being close to an express engine just as it starts—the booming was gradual and slow, went on increasing in intensity and rapidity, until it became so insupportable, that she was often compelled to go and lie down, to try and get respite in sleep. In other instances, deafness in one ear, palpitations, or at least irregular action of the heart, with a sense of weight over the forehead, have occurred; and when warm in bed, the skin has itched, together with cramps and numbness in one or more limbs. The period at which the attacks appear, or are aggravated, is worthy of notice; when the sufferer from them does not get up under their influence, they will occur probably in the after part of the day, and become increased if a sense of hunger ensues, which is not speedily gratified. In nearly all such instances, there is flatulence, constipation, and a capricious appetite. The expulsion of sour or fetid wind from the stomach, followed by instant relief to the head, has given rise to the idea of its being "wind in the head." These distressing feelings are continually mistaken for apoplectic or epileptic seizures; at any rate, they are too often treated as symptoms of excess of blood in the head, and recourse is had to a lowering regimen, purgative medicine, and even leeches, &c., to the temples; but these measures invariably add to the distress, and increase the sufferings of the patient.

Many incredulous persons will stare with astonishment at the suggestion, that such severe symptoms as those now related may arise from the abuse of tea drinking, and will reply, that men should therefore be equally affected with women. The explanation of this difference is found in the fact, that neither men nor women would suffer, if the skin were forced to carry off a large quantity of moisture; but as women are sedentary, and men active in their employments, so the latter escape, whilst the former suffer.

FOURTH STAGE.

YOUNG MEN TO MEN.

TWENTY-ONE TO TWENTY-EIGHT YEARS.

CHAPTER XII.

Bread—Beer—Spirits—Intoxicating Drinks—The "horrors" and fruits of Intemperance; Gout and Gravel, Pimples and Blotches, Nettle Rash, Worms, and Giddiness.

EVERY lover of good "home-made bread" ought to know that alum is not only unnecessary to our existence—and is, therefore, not met with in our animal composition—but that it produces injurious effects upon our system when introduced into it by means of bread. The fact is, that a gross error exists in the minds of the higher and middle classes, viz., that white bread is purer than a darker sort; whereas, in almost every case, the former is aluminated, and the latter is non-aluminated bread. Wheat, before it gets into the hands of the baker, may have begun to sprout; its starch is thereby in course of conversion into sugar. Such flour would form sticky, dirty-looking bread; but the introduction of alum stops this process, renders the bread white, and deceives the consumer into a belief that it is made of pure wheaten flour. The result is more or less injurious to the stomach. The sweet principle in bread fattens, and hence great bread eaters have usually a tendency to corpulence ; but they are by no means so obese as great beer and spirit drinkers. In this kind of beverage, the saccharine principle is converted into alcohol ; and, whilst the former fattens, the enervating effect of the latter is, alas! too well known amongst us. But though a hard-working, free-perspiring beer-drinker may live to a good old age, the sedentary dram-tippler is soon overtaken with disordered stomach, weak digestion, restless nights—until all the miseries of an attack of " the horrors " come on ; to relieve which, he will, if possible, keep himself in a constant state of semi-intoxication, until the real disease, " delirium tremens " renders him a temporary maniac, of the most wild and ungovernable character. It is a pitiable sight to witness a naturally kind and well-disposed man utterly wrecked in body and in mind by drink. The character of the patient usually comes out in broad features under his temporary delusions. I once attended a coachman from one of our great West-end livery stables. In his delirium his whole time was occupied in driving a four-in-hand break from the stables into the City. You might easily follow him through the streets, as he had a remark to make upon every house, building, shop, or turning. He held the reins (so to speak) in his hand, and with the whip in the other, he mounted the box, saying, " Good-bye," to Jim ; and " Hold the off leader," to another., On getting out of the stable-yard into the street, his whole attention was evidently taken up with this " pretty off leader," which he described to us as " a high spirited creature, full of play and of blood ;" but she made a shy at something, and nearly drove the break against the wall. At this (supposed) event, he became very excited and eager ; and calling the master, who, in his imagination, stood near, explained the matter to him. When fairly out into the streets, he continued to halloo at the horses : coaxing one, talking kindly to another, and growling at the " off leader." The actions in his supposed driving, the rapid and quaint observations as he passed down one street into another, his remarks upon the beautiful team, his jokes, and extreme mental anguish to get on and keep all safe, exceeded everything I had ever witnessed. He evidently dreaded the City and St. Paul's Churchyard.* Here the " off leader," in turning into the yard, " shied ;" in another moment, he was against the curbstone, and "the beautiful creature" was on the pavement. I can never forget the agony of the poor man. The perspiration, the vociferating language, the agitation, nay, horror, of his mind at such a (supposed) calamity—the busy, eager, and fierce glare of his eye and face—told too plainly the reality of his distress ; and in a few hours more he sank exhausted under this trial to his incoherent mind. Alas ! poor fellow, his case is as vivid to my mind at this moment as though I had just left him, though fifteen years have gone by.

It is extremely rare to meet with this frightful result of dram-drinking in our female population, yet they are in many districts as much given up to the vice as men; but there is a striking analogy between that female disease, hysteria, and the drunkard's " horrors," in this fact, that entire loss of consciousness never occurs in either of them. In an hysterical fit, the patient knows what is said, though she may not, or will not, reply to questions put to her. And so, also, in delirium tremens. The patient, far from being taciturn, will so smartly reply to every question you ask him, that by a little care, a bystander may keep up a tolerably connected gossip for a quarter of an hour. In the midst of his loquacity, the Doctor may stop him by suddenly and authoritatively accosting him thus, " Put out your tongue, sir !" " Where do you live ?" &c.; but should a nurse venture to use such language, she will be met by some such reply as " Who made you a doctor, miss ?"

After witnessing a few of such harrowing effects of drink as the one now related, the most fastidious person and powerful opponent of a temperance society would become a convert, it is hoped, to the proposition that " all liquors are deleterious in our ordinary healthy condition ; and that pure water, toast-and-water, milk, whey,

* The reverberation of sound in this churchyard produces a striking contrast to the incessant din going on in the streets; and we gathered that this was the ground of his fear.

and other unexciting beverages, would be preferable, if we could only
consent, in early life, to deny ourselves further indulgence." Unless
the habit is begun and encouraged at an early period, the practice
is scarcely salutary in after life, when the system is become habit-
uated to a certain quantity of alcoholic stimulants.

Men, when they approach the meridian of life, or are about to
descend the scale, are like children before they arrive at puberty,
they become very sensible of those periodical alternations of the year,
" Spring and Fall." If dram-drinking amongst the lower classes
fosters " the horrors," the indulgence in wine or malt liquor
encourages the disposition to gout in the higher classes. This tendency exhibits itself more when the seasons are unsettled, that is,
when warm weather is abruptly followed by much moisture, and this
is succeeded by severe cold nights, as in Autumn; the skin becomes
checked in its secretion, and the fluids of the system are not thrown
off, and gout is engendered. The early steps towards this habit of
body in wine and beer-drinkers may be thus traced :—In the first
place, the individual suffers from impaired appetite, heartburn,
flatulence, and even sickness. Strange cramps fly about the frame,
and when the patient can " throw up " a little sour wind, the pains
are easier. The mental depression is sometimes painfully great, and
the worst forebodings are indulged in. Now, although such symptoms disappear after a severe fit of gout, yet many persons get
relief without going through this painful ordeal. You may generate
gout, feed it, and at length bring it forth, with all its pains and
penalties. For when a gouty tendency is born with a man, certain
habits of indulgence in animal food, beer, and much wine, will
eventually give rise to the attack: but, on the other hand, the
disease, or its tendency, may be kept in abeyance for life by careful
and strict attention to rules of diet—unless the innate or constitutional disposition to an attack is very strong ; and when that is the
case, " the bite of a flea will excite an attack," as related by Dr.
Heberden.

The burly face has become proverbially associated with intemperance ; whilst the " flushings " of certain females, from forty to fifty

years of age, have been unkindly construed into the same cause. Nothing can be more unjust and untrue. The blotches, black spots, and pimples, on the forehead, cheeks, &c., of some young people, especially boys, are easily removed by plain living, &c., &c.; but the more obstinate forms of "pimpled face," or of "flushings," are not so manageable. It is often hereditary, and is usually seen in persons who inherit gout from their parents or grandsire.

Another poison the human stomach has frequently to grapple with through injudicious diet, is met with in tainted fish. Summer itching, increased by eating fruit, may give rise to tingling of the hands and arms; but this animal poison is generally resented by an attack of nettle rash. The worst form of the kind I ever witnessed occurred in a respectable mechanic, who had been to a supper party, where three different kinds of fish were on the table. He partook of each; and in less than an hour he became giddy, his face swelled and tingled, and the severest vomiting ensued, which could not be controlled for twenty hours. This man became "a martyr to indigestion" for months afterwards, until he was persuaded to live upon spoon food for several weeks, when he ultimately got well. Cucumbers, mushrooms, or a draught of senna tea, but especially muscles, crabs, and prawns, will produce the attack in some persons. The only resource in such cases is to clear the stomach by means of an emetic, followed by an antacid aperient, and to pay a strict attention to diet, under medical supervision.

The public, as well as the profession, have sometimes the greatest difficulty in dissociating certain feelings in the head—such as giddiness, noises, dimness of sight, and even numbness of one arm, &c.—from a threatened apoplectic seizure, or an approaching attack of paralysis; though the stomach, or liver, or both, may be, in many instances, the seat of the disturbance.

It will not be here out of place to mention that similar feelings may exist in an otherwise healthy person, from the presence of Entozoa in the alimentary canal. A tall, robust man, was under treatment some time ago with the following singular attack. His features were expressionless, there was a dulness of physiognomy, and he complained of partial dimness of the *left* eye ; the iris was active and natural. He had numbness extending down the right arm and leg, and over the left side of the face ; he was so giddy that he was afraid to trust himself to walk across the street. Sometimes the numbness was so severe, that he could not put the foot to the ground. The treatment he had undergone convinced me that the medical man had taken the same view of the symptoms that I should probably have done. He had been cupped, blistered, &c., without the slightest benefit. The first suspicion that the distress was not seated in the head, but that it was referred to that spot by some eccentric irritation far removed from it, arose from the circumstance, that the numbness would suddenly leave one arm and attack the opposite. In the midst of this perplexity, the patient became convalescent in a few weeks, by a series of anthelminctic remedies.

FIFTH STAGE.

MEN.

TWENTY-EIGHT TO FORTY-NINE YEARS.

CHAPTER XIII.

Healthful harmony of Stomach, Heart, and Lungs—Asthma or Stomach Cough, and its Freaks—The Liver a helpmate to the Stomach—Its duties and disorders—Jaundice—Bilious Headaches, their treachery and obscurity—Hypochondriacs and their eccentricities.

It need not be a matter of surprise that the lungs of a man, that is to say, his breathing apparatus, should sympathize with derangement in the duties of the stomach, when we are informed that the same track of nervous fibres supplying the one organ affords nerves to the other, and that the whole system of heart, lungs, and stomach are thereby intimately blended together, and are in unison one with another, in health and in disease. The most singular freaks are often exhibited by that wonderful nerve (pneumo-gastric), when it is deranged in its mysterious operations; the "nervous spasmodic" complaints that ensue are very inexplicable. In no derangement do we witness such peculiarity more than in asthma. One person afflicted with this complaint dares not expose himself to the dust of ipecacuanha-powder, without incurring the risk of having a fearful seizure of breathlessness, whilst another may do so with impunity.

A farmer from the neighbourhood of Bristol always found relief in his severest attacks of asthma, if he could reach a certain hotel in Tooley Street, London Bridge.

Dr. Watson relates a still more singular instance. A gentleman at Cambridge could sleep in the "Red Lion Inn," but not in the "Eagle;" if at Paris, and he slept in "Hôtel Meurice" front, he was safe; if at the back, he never escaped a fit; and whilst Dover Street, Piccadilly, agreed with him, Clarges Street (a stone's throw from it) never did. Manchester Square was a torture to him, because he said it was built upon piles! Many such cases are on record, which wholly baffle explanation. One came under my notice during the winter of 1859-60. The subject of it was a foreman to a business in a large city market; his age was forty-three; and he had been suffering from attacks of asthma for eighteen years, so that, to use his wife's own words, they both were resigned to the certainty that an attack would shortly carry him off. He had become much shattered in his frâme, and was now unable to work more than three or four days out of the week. He had been under various kinds of treatment, with some temporary benefit, but had never lost his seizures. The first thing that struck my mind, as he conversed about his maladies, was the entire loss of every tooth but one in his head, the stumps of many alone remained. His stomach was much enfeebled in its powers, and he was dieted accordingly, and tonic medicines prescribed. A note was taken of every seizure, from the first time he came under my observation, and at the end of four months, though he was somewhat relieved, he had had some sharp seizures at longer intervals; these intervals were accurately timed, and it was now observed that the attacks invariably returned on a Saturday or Sunday night; in short, he had always six days' respite, and his wife and friends had remarked that Sunday usually found him an invalid. He was urged to see a dentist, and he submitted to have all the stumps extracted, and an entire new set of teeth put in; and in this state he improved in strength, with a gradual cessation of the asthma—but on each Saturday he was directed to take a full dose of quinine every four hours during the day. From that time to the present day (twenty-two months), he has never had a single seizure, and an insurance-office has consented " to take up " his life, as he now looks the picture of health. This is one of the most singular, and at the same time the most gratifying instances of a cure of a serious malady, that ever came under my notice, through attention to the wants, trials, and troubles of a weak stomach and impaired digestion.

Nocturnal attacks of spasmodic disease are much more frequent than diurnal seizures, and the explanation must be sought for in the fact, that the pulse becomes slower every evening at nightfall, and that it resumes its accustomed rapidity at dawn. Nervous influence is at its lowest ebb in the " dead " of the night, and it reaches its maximum power at noon. In febrile diseases, especially in children, it always augurs an unfavourable sign when the day is passed in dozing, and the night in wanderings, sleeplessness, and fever; the reverse of these phenomena are the surest tokens of returning health.

The most refreshing sleep in our twenty-four hours' cycle, is that obtained between the hours of ten and three; the whole frame is then under the least possible excitement; and, as day dawns, the system is gradually roused to watchfulness by the returning activity of the circulation. The feathered tribes, with their heads buried beneath the wing, are roused from their roost by the increased stimulus of the blood on the retina and brain, before the dawn approaches, and *not* by light beaming on their delicate organs of vision at sunrise.

Some individuals become feverish and ill with every return of the hay season, though they may be removed miles from the fields. A colleague of mine was annually an invalid for a week or more, when the hay-making time came on around Hampstead and Highgate; the distance from his rooms to the fields exceeded three miles.

Beneath those two portions of our body where laughter is represented as " holding both her sides," we find the liver on the right, and the spleen on the left. Here it is that the stomach reigns as prime minister of the whole cavity, and its most important helpmate is the liver.

F

This gland, like every other organ in our frame, is nourished by arterial (red) blood, which returns to the heart again as venous (black) fluid; but, besides this, there is a special arrangement of the blood vessels, in which are contained bile-making constituents, derived from the digested food in the alimentary canal, so that, with its three sets of blood-vessels, its gall-bladder, and bile-ducts, it is a signally curious and wonderful appendage to the digestive apparatus. We can always estimate the relative value of the several organs of our body, by comparing their presence and functions with similar organs in the lower vertebrates. It has been already stated that some kind of stomach is found in the lowest link of the animal world ; next in importance to it is the liver, so that, whether it be an aquatic or an air-breathing animal, yet some provision exists for the purpose of forming bile, and aiding in the all-important processes of digestion, nutrition, and growth. As soon as the food we swallow is fitted to make its exit from the stomach, it meets with the bile. This agent converts the nutrient mass into chyle, the food of the blood; the solvent juice of the stomach is not more important in digestion therefore than the presence of healthy bile in that portion of the canal immediately below the stomach, into which the bile flows. This subtle and all-dissolving fluid serves many other purposes : it stimulates the whole alimentary tube to a constant vermicular motion ; it preserves the blood from contamination ; for if the principles of bile remain untaken away from the system, the circulation soon evinces the fruit of its presence. The brain and nerves, no longer supplied and nourished by health-giving blood, flag in the execution of their duties ; the mental powers are enfeebled ; the sensitiveness of the individual to trifling misfortunes is increased ; and both body and mind are prostrated through the depressing influence of bile in the system, as it is popularly designated. Under these disturbing causes, the patient is troubled with a visionary or exaggerated sense of pains, lowness of spirits, groundless apprehension of personal troubles ; peculiar trains of ideas haunt the imagination and overwhelm the judgment; misanthropy, weariness of life, and a spleenful frame of mind often follow each other.

It is pitiable to witness the human mind succumbing to these influences. Any shock to the mental faculties may lead to them; but none is so powerful an agent as disappointment; hence it is that we meet with many instances of this kind amongst the weaker sex, after they have received some blight to their prospects in life. Yes, but even the wisest and best of mankind are as open to this affliction as the weakest.

The writer once knew a highly-intelligent woman of secluded and sedentary habits, whose life, for fifteen years of it, was one scene of vexation and disappointment, because she believed herself betrothed to an illustrious duke, who, beyond giving a reply to certain communications sent to him, had never fed such an hallucination, and the bubble did not burst until after his death, when she retired from all society, secreted herself from friends, and no one was suffered to ascertain her place of abode. She had spent the greater part of her income in providing rooms lavishly furnished for the reception of her guest, whilst she denied herself the ordinary comforts of home and of sustenance. "Such persons are usually of a testy frame of mind, distrustful, peevish, apt to mistake and ready to snarl upon every occasion, and without any cause, with their dearest friends. If they speak in jest, the patient takes it in good earnest; if the smallest ceremony be accidentally omitted, the poor creature is wounded to the quick."* It is in this species of mental disturbance that much may be done in relieving the sufferers by a proper course of medicine. The liver has become sluggish, the system torpid, the blood is imperfectly deprived of the constituents of bile, and this agent re-acts as a poisonous dose on the brain and nervous system. Many persons who have been awfully tempted to commit self-destruction, have become relieved of their horrible feelings by a few smart doses of blue pill and black draught, with a thin spare diet; after which, a tonic plan of treatment, cheerful society, and intellectual employment, with open-air exercise, especially equestrian, have been the means of restoring a healthy tone of mind and of body.

* Burton.

F 2

Well authenticated instances of jaundice are on record, that have occurred on the perusal of a letter containing distressing news. A father of a family, once under my care, became jaundiced on the loss of his wife and two children by scarlet fever. He recovered in a fortnight after active purgation. A young physician, of my acquaintance, was similarly affected, during the progress of study for his examination. He ably acquitted himself on the day of his trial, and in a brief period afterwards his mind regained its healthy elasticity, and the complaint disappeared. A valued relative once embarked in an undertaking which might have rendered him comparatively penniless, or from which he expected to realize some hundreds of pounds. Although he had enjoyed excellent health prior to this anxious enterprise, yet now he became intensely jaundiced, and remained so three months, in spite of a large quantity of medicine which he took. He was so vividly yellow, that he was known under the sobriquet of " The Prince of Orange." As the business in which he had embarked compelled him to appear in public, he was the more anxious to obtain a natural hue to his features, but it was all in vain. The week of trial arrived, and on Thursday evening the whole business was satisfactorily arranged, and his expectations realized. He went to bed with a cheerful spirit, and on Saturday morning his family could scarcely trace a vestige of jaundice in his countenance. He has enjoyed excellent health from that time, though thirty-six years have elapsed since the occurrence.

One of the most common ailments, "flesh is heir to," passes under the name of bilious, or sick headache. Palpitation of the heart, an inordinate craving or sinking at the stomach, restless nights and disagreeable dreams often precede such attacks. Flatulence, with a sense of nausea in the mouth on rising, accompany these feelings. The very best management of such symptoms, in a person who lives freely and enjoys health, is to proclaim a few days' fast, and not to postpone medical treatment, lest a more serious attack supervene. It is often a source of flattery to the fast declining powers of a consumptive individual, that he gets thin because he

suffers from so much indigestion and biliousness. Alas! poor creature, he mistakes cause for effect; the deranged stomach and liver
are the consequence of lung disease, and in the improvement of the
latter, the former also become relieved. A sister of a medical man
lost all relish for animal food during many months, and if she were
prevailed on to take some, it usually brought on severe cough, until
the meal was rejected. She had cough at no other time than on first
rising in the morning; so that, as the appetite quite failed, the gradual
wasting of the body did not surprise her or her relatives. She was
constantly bilious in her feelings and took large quantities of medicine for supposed liver disorder: but at length she was reluctantly
induced to consult a physician. I then found unequivocal evidence
of advanced consumption; she was removed to a relative in France,
where she died in six weeks after the discovery of this insidious
lung disease, a victim to long-continued self-management and mis-
understanding of a fatal disorder.

A very similar occurrence happened during the last year. A
master carpenter was the subject of constant cough and nausea
after food, whilst at other times he was able to work and lead an
active life. His teeth were much decayed, and many were quite
gone, although he was only forty years of age. He grew weak
from mal-nourishment. He was desired to see a dentist, and a
particular line of diet, with tonic and other medicines, were prescribed, and he ultimately lost both nausea and cough, although
there was no doubt that each depended on tubercular disease of
the lung. He was the father of the lad whose case of epileptic
seizures is mentioned at page 39.

SIXTH STAGE.

ELDERLY MEN.

FORTY-NINE TO SEVENTY YEARS.

CHAPTER XIV.

Life's Great Climacteric Epoch—Singular and Curious Metamorphoses—
Brittleness of Bone in the Aged, and their Tendency to Fractures.

" THE days of our years are three score years and ten," and this
duration of life has undergone no change from the Patriarchal age
to the present moment. The Greek physiologists reckoned five
epochs only in man's life, beginning with the 7th year ; they deter-
mined that as the 1st climacteric period—the 2nd was 3 times 7 ;
the 3rd, 7 times 7 ; the 4th, 9 times seven ; and the 5th, 9 times 9.
The two last were designated grand climacterics, in which life was
supposed to have consummated itself. The change which frequently strikes our notice as taking place, during the period here
referred to, is of two kinds. A wonderful renovation of power, or
else a sudden decay of strength. In the former, deaf people re-
cover their hearing, weak sight no longer requires spectacles,
some newly-formed teeth are cut, the hair evinces a similar regeneration, grows again, or is restored to its pristine colour ; and
the whole man is made young again. On the other hand, a sudden
breaking up of the system may ensue, and the individual abruptly

sink into a state of general decay. In this instance, medical aid may be of essential service, on the application of which we may observe the powers of life, as in other diseases, rally and become invigorated down to a good old age. This degeneration, at the climacteric period of life, gradually and insensibly comes on. We are now arrived at that state of transition in which our various tissues undergo some kind of transformation. Women, more frequently than men, grow fat, with shortness of breath, attended by a pale, flabby skin. Certain parts of the body are " cast off because their component elements die, as in the case of hair—death at the hair-bulb precedes the falling off of the hair ;"* so also the removal of the fang of a tooth is the result of a degeneration of its parts, before the tooth itself falls out. The same laws influence the decadence of life ; by a curious substitution, fat now takes the place of muscles, glands, and even bones. Diseased growths not unfrequently present themselves also at this eventful period of life, and tend to destroy the healthy parts around them. Organs, which have now ceased to take an active part in the *rôle* of man's reproduction or nutrition, are most liable to be the seat of this maltransformation. But the most interesting, *natural* decay in man, is to be met with in the skeleton of his body. A salt of phosphorus is necessary to our bones. We get this phosphate of lime from our meat and vegetable diet, whilst the sheep and oxen get it from the herbage they feed on. In the bones of man there are cells, the 2,000th of an inch in diameter ; into these cells the globules of blood, 3-500th part of an inch in diameter, pass for nutrition.

As the climacteric period of life draws on, these cells become filled with bony matter, and the whole skeleton is progressively consolidated during the remainder of life. Hence, a physiologist can readily distinguish the various bones of an old from those of a young animal.

The brittleness of bone in old persons, and their readiness to become fractured on the least injury, is thus explained ; but if an

---

* On Nutrition, by James Paget, Esq., 1847.

aged person is capable of taking much out-door exercise, the continual waste of tissue that is caused thereby preserves the bones from this brittleness. The writer has been told of a man upwards of fourscore, who walks six miles, three times a week, to his work as a blacksmith. In him, such a change of bone would be very much retarded.

· The regeneration of tissue being no longer demanded, this bony matter is not only spread out over the whole area of the skeleton, but in due time it is met with on the inner coats of the heart and main arteries, especially those within the skull, giving rise to two common sources of sudden death—heart disease, and brain disease, or apoplexy.

This subject is replete with interest as contrasted with the equally marvellous reparative power displayed in bone when destroyed by disease, or fractured by accident. The "new fabric then gradually becomes perfectly continuous with the old, progressively acquiring the form and solidity of the original bone."* It will be observed, therefore, that as life decays, the blow it receives is mainly felt in two of the most important organs of the frame; the one, that nicely balanced hydraulic engine—the heart, presiding over our animal existence; the other—the mind, that noble part of man, wherein resides his intellectual and moral powers. When one or both of these pillars of the fabric begin to crumble, it is not to be wondered at if the whole structure of him who was created in the Divine Image should soon totter and fall to its mother earth and dust.

But, as age advances, not only may the body suddenly grow corpulent, but the person may, perhaps, "make fat" inwardly, whilst his outward appearance presents little alteration. Every one is familiar with the dairyman's method of fattening poultry, or with the "Smithfield Cattle Show-men's" process of getting the beasts to "lay on" as much fat, in a short time, as will insure the admiration of the breeder, and gain the prize of the society. We should be shocked at the subtle dodges which these persons resort

* "Carpenter's Physiology," and "Sharpey's Development of Bone."

to, in order to fatten their stock, but man, with his bad habits of full diet, want of exercise, seclusion from society and from fresh air, may be classed with the Dorking fowl, the Essex duck, and the Strasbourg goose, whose "*foie gras*" supply the *patés* held in such high estimation by epicures. The most distressing family troubles are brought about by these bad indulgences; the mind becomes indolent, the temper irritable, and the least disturbing cause is likely to throw a female into fits of hysteria, as, in one instance, a woman lost her voice for fifteen years; or give a gouty subject a fit of gravel, if not gout. When I was a student, there resided in the same town a relative of mine, who was a shrewd, observing woman. In the circle of her acquaintance was an unmarried lady just past the prime of life, who had suffered from "fits" of an equivocal character from time to time. My friend gave her an invitation to pass a few weeks at her house, which was accepted, but very shortly afterwards these "fits" exhibited themselves, to the great annoyance of her hostess. However, as they recurred again and again, and did not cause any distress to the sufferer, they excited no alarm. At length, on one occasion, when the visitor went to lie down preparatory to a fit, her hostess seized the opportunity by saying, " Well, my dear Miss ——, if you are going to have a fit to-day, I'll lock you up in your bed-room, and go out and spend the day with Mr. —— and his wife," which she did, and took the key with her, and returned to her patient in the evening, whom she found quite well, but highly chagrined at the treatment she had received. Nevertheless, " the fits " were cured, and no one heard any more of them during her protracted residence in the town. Had a medical man exercised this apparently cruel treatment, he would doubtless have received his *congé* immediately.

Such strange attacks in women of riper years, whose experience of life is matured, and who possess intelligent minds, are very humiliating. The seizures are not wholly wilful, neither are they wholly uncontrollable; but in the majority of instances, sedentary habits have induced sluggishness of liver and weak digestion, and they require to be constantly roused by mental and bodily dissipation, or they merge into a misanthropical state, and a premature senile weakness of mind and body comes on.   One of the most suspicious cases of the kind occurred in a woman who had been bed-ridden for nine years, and which is quoted by my kind and valued friend, Dr. Watson.*   The patient had been under the care of various . ledical gentlemen, some of whom had a doubt of the nature of the helplessness.   Several ladies and gentlemen in the neigh-bourhood of Regent's Park contributed most kindly and lavishly to her support, during the whole period of her bed-ridden state.   She was at length watched and nursed in the hospital by a sensible, firm, though kind nurse, who aided us in trying to move her legs, and, to the surprise of all, in ten days she succeeded in getting her to walk down the ward, leaning only on the attendant's arm, and in three weeks more she was walking alone in the hospital garden.   The effects of this rapid recovery on the minds of the relations proved that some secret collusion had been indulged in, for they went round to the benevolent persons who had supported her, and related the most vicious untruths respecting the treatment the woman had received ; but when these kind friends sought out the real facts of the case, and saw the person in rude health, walking about the ward, they were indignant at the imposition, and very properly withdrew all support from the former deluded cripple.

* " Lectures on Principles and Practice of Medicine," Art. " Hysteria."

SIXTH STAGE.

ELDERLY MEN.

FORTY-NINE TO SEVENTY YEARS.

CHAPTER XV.

The Heart; its Troubles and Difficulties; Fat, Lean, and degenerate Hearts —" Breast Pang;" its Character and Treatment—Irritable Hearts and fretful Tempers.

REFERENCE has been already made to the fact, that spare persons will often grow corpulent as they enter the first great climacteric of declining years; namely, forty-nine to seventy. When active exercise or employment ceases, and with it the demand for the supply caused by the usual " wear and tear" of the animal machine, it is no uncommon event to find the elements once consumed in the vital working of our frames now stored up in portions of the body, where they, in course of time, serve as fetters or bands to the future progress of the machine, whilst decay and death are the results of this accumulation. In this case, the heart also is one of the earliest organs to suffer, fat is distributed around it, in lieu of serving as fuel for animal heat or combustion, and a fat heart is necessarily a weak heart, and this feebleness of action induces other disturbances in the general health.

It is singular to remark, how instinctively elderly persons avoid those articles of diet which contain much fat, and are, therefore,

difficult of digestion. Pork is said to contain fifty, and veal only
sixteen per cent. of fat ; and amongst fish, herrings possess the most,
and soles the least oil. Animal heat in advanced life is better sus-
tained by starchy than by oily food, the former is readily converted
into sugar, and thus becomes a good heating material, whilst fat
must be submitted to a more intricate process, analogous to soap
making, ere it can enter the system, and be serviceable to the
economy as fat. We find persons in advanced life fond of light,
farinaceous puddings, they avoid the fat meats of the butcher's shop,
and prefer poultry, game or fish. A slow heart is attended with
slow breathing, and feeble circulation ; and the hands and feet are
prone to be easily chilled ; a quick heart, on the other hand, keeps
pace with more frequent breathing, a warm skin, and an active
glow in the extremities. The infant heart at birth, starts into life
at the rate of 120 beats per minute , the septuagenarian's heart has
reduced its throbs to one-ha :, and the diminution in these sixty con-
tractions is greatest from infancy to the second dentition, after
which period, it averages 80 from puberty to manhood, and then
gradually verges to 60 per minute until death. The number of
respirations per minute may be calculated on as 30 in the infantile,
and 15 in the elderly man, or one-fourth less than the heart's action
throughout life.

It is reasonable to expect that if a person rapidly fattens, the
heart may become involved in the same excess of fat, but there
is a far more insidious, and, therefore, more important change in
this organ, which has arrested the attention of medical men, within
these few years, in consequence of its nature and results having
been clearly pointed out by a few eminent pathologists who have
devoted much labour to the subject. In the old bills of mortality,
one great item of causes of death was commonly denominated by
the unmeaning term " rising of the lights," and under this head
was included all instances of sudden death. Doubtless the cause
now under notice, formed a good proportion of such deaths. The
change in the heart referred to has been found in the majority of
instances to take place after sixty years of age. The patient may

have shown evidences of fattening, but with this increase there will be also a pale, sickly cast in the general appearance, with a sear leaf pallor of the face ; any hasty ascent or exertion, brings on a breathlessness ; frequent yawnings before and after meals, slowness in the pulse, coldness in the extremities, and listlessness of mind, are the usual accompaniments of this change in the heart ; yet, as Mr. Paget truly remarks, " such persons are fit enough for all the ordinary events of calm and quiet life, but are wholly unable to resist the storm of a sickness, an accident, or an operation." In eighty-three cases recorded by Dr. Quain of this change, sixty-eight died suddenly, and doubtless the instances of death from a " rupture, or broken heart," in George II., and his relative, the Duchess of Brunswick, with two eminent men in our day (Drs. Chalmers and Abercrombie), arose from the same fatal change in this organ. In all the instances that have come under my observation, it has been found that special forms of tonic medicine have greatly relieved the persons suspected to be labouring under this disorder. The writer is strongly impressed with the belief, that the lamented Prince Consort was the subject of this change in the structure of the heart. It is scarcely necessary to add, that temperance, calmness, and evenness of temper, are essential to the comfort of such sufferers.

One singular whim very common to old men in the higher walks of life, is the determination to keep up the habits of youth ; they will breakfast moderately at nine, and take nothing again until the dinner hour at six or seven. Now as breakfast, after a refreshing night's rest, is digested more quickly than any subsequent meal, the stomach is left unemployed from noon until six o'clock, and if the person eats heartily at dinner, the period of digestion having been so long postponed, the operation is now more tardy and more difficult ; the re-action upon a weak heart, brings on a sudden cessation of its functions, and hence it is, that death from heart disease commonly takes place after long fasting, or soon after a full meal. Yet with all this, a mortal disease may afflict a man and that disease not destroy life, until old age, though he may have been exposed to innumerable chances of death.

What an impenetrable mystery is the fathomless depth of Divine Providence, with its secret wheel within wheel. Comforted under the sacred assurance that, by His Almighty management, all things work together for good, we may assure ourselves that we are—

> " Safe in the hand of One disposing power,
> Or in the natal, or the mortal hour,
> All nature is but art, unknown to thee,
> All chance, direction which thou canst not see."

A celebrated general enters the British army as a youth, rises through the several gradations of his profession, is in active service in the Peninsular campaigns, at Waterloo, in the Crimea, and lastly in India, returns to his native shore, unscathed, and dies suddenly in a London omnibus, at the age of seventy-eight, after he had left his club to join his family dinner-party. Such was the case of Sir H. G——. He had suffered from "breast pang" for a few years before his death, but, like an old soldier, would never complain or seek advice for it, until the enfeebled heart came to a sudden arrest in its power, whilst the stomach was under the influence of long-fasting. The nutrient arteries of the heart were like bits of coral, so advanced was their conversion into bony matter.

The disease now alluded to—" the breast pang"—was another ancient item of sudden death from " rising of the lights." It has been remarked that when an elderly person, who has completed his grand climacteric (sixty-three), complains of a sense of strangling, seizing him in a moment, and giving rise to an uncontrollable alarm, in fact, to a dread of instant death, that such a person is most probably the subject of the disease, especially if with this distress there is also a painful fulness, or disagreeable plunging sensation through the left breast, and which, if severe, shakes the whole frame, perspiration bursts forth, slight faintness comes over him, and in a few minutes the attack passes off. These dire symptoms are sure to be brought on by any exertion, or in ascending the stairs, &c. Two eminent ministers were walking together a few years ago up a hill, one was twenty years younger than the other, but the elder was the subject of this heart complaint, and every ten or fifteen paces, he was compelled to stand still for a few moments to get breath ; the younger pooh-poohed it, saying, " I tell you, man, it's all nervousness ; come along, and walk it off." In a few years the old man died, under the influence of this disease ; and the younger has also since fallen under the same, but not until he learnt, by much suffering, how erroneously he interpreted the breathlessness of his beloved friend, who had gone before him. In this disease there is usually little or no shortness of breath; in two cases now under my care, the persons, both men, are instantaneously seized, and to witness the attack is the clearest evidence one can receive of the nature of the complaint. In the majority of instances of heart disease, I have observed that the patients have been more than usually subject to fits of anger, peevishness, or ill temper ; in short, some have complained that their disposition had become so irritable, that they had quite lost their former character of possessing mild and amiable tempers. Indigestion, more or less severe, is sure to be a constant source of trouble also in this complaint. The utmost precaution must be observed, therefore, in the character of diet, and the general state of the alimentary canal ; above all, the patient must deny himself active employment, especially after food ; nor should he expose himself to sudden fits of anger or mental worry. A raw medical student, on first visiting the wards of our hospitals, and hearing the various tales of suffering from the poor, is often led to suppose that diseases of this organ are more frequent amongst the Irish than others, since they are always complaining of " pain at the heart." A witty physician once corrected such ignorance, by stating that you may always expect to hear a Scotchman complain of a " sair head ;" an Irishman, of a " pain at his heart ;" whilst John Bull, when ailing, is afraid of being "starved to death."

SIXTH STAGE.

ELDERLY MEN.

FORTY-NINE TO SEVENTY YEARS.

CHAPTER XVI.

Recreations and exercises for preserving health—Mental toil, and its evils, Sir H. Davy—Bodily exercises and its abuses, Dr. Samuel Johnson—Flutterings—Smoking—Use and abuse of the "Deadly Night-shade" family.

WALKING is, perhaps, the readiest mode of taking exercise, and the one most extensively resorted to by us all; whilst riding may be classed amongst the most active forms, since it requires much exertion of the whole frame, and where it is practicable is very useful to persons advanced in life. But the abuse of these healthy occupations for exercise consists in taking them when the system is exhausted more or less by previous fasting or by mental labour. Some persons injudiciously attempt a long walk before breakfast, under the belief that it is conducive to health. Others will get up early to work three hours at some abstruse mental toil. The effect in both instances is the same; it subtracts from the powers of exertion in the after part of the day. A short saunter, or some light reading before this meal, is the best indulgence of the kind; otherwise the waste occasioned by labour must be supplied by nourishment, and the breakfast will necessarily become a heavy meal, and the whole morning's comfort sacrificed by a weight at the chest from imperfect digestion of food. These observations apply especially to elderly persons who are prone to flatter themselves into the persuasion that they can use their mental or bodily powers in age as in youth. Numerous instances are on record, of intense mental study cutting short a valuable life, particularly where one subject has been ardently pursued, as in the case of Sir Humphry Davy, who spent the greater part of the day in his laboratory, until the appointed dinner hour had passed. He would resume his chemical labours until three or four in the morning, and yet the servant, not unfrequently, found he had risen before him.* Poor Weber's mournful exclamation, in the midst of his numerous engagements cannot be easily forgotten, "Would that I were a tailor, for then I should have a Sunday holiday!" The contrast in the life and pursuits of Davy with those of Lords Brougham and Palmerston is remarkable. The enormous powers of labour in the former, and versatility of talent in the latter, have been a topic of conversation, and a matter of surprise, for the last twenty-five years. But, as Burton wisely observed, the body is "domicilium animæ," the home, abode, and stay of the soul; and, "as a torch gives a better light and a sweeter smell according to the matter it is made of, so doth our soul perform all her actions better or worse, as her organs are disposed; or, as wine savours of the cask wherein it is kept, the soul receives a tincture from the body, through which it works."

The constitution of the natural world around us is in harmony also with this healthy condition of man. The gifts of Providence are unavailable unless the surface of the earth is tilled by manual labour, and mental exertion is as essential to our social comforts as bodily exercise is to our health. But, as the ground must have its succession of crops to preserve it in a fruitful condition, and its terms of fallow or rest, so mental, as well as bodily, labour must have its changes and hours of repose.

* "Biography of Sir H. Davy," by Dr. Paris.

There is nothing under the sun which will pleasingly engage our thoughts for any considerable length of time, but that something inferior will invariably be preferred, if it be only new. · An eminent physiologist, not long dead, when he had been engaged for six or eight hours in hard mental toil, found that he derived the greatest relaxation by strolling down Regent-street, Piccadilly, and other thoroughfares, reading the names, &c., over the houses as he walked along. A barrister informed me that one of our most acute judges was employed lately in a very abstruse case, and had sat seven or eight hours in court, until he became "misty" in his mental powers; a country gentleman of his acquaintance stood at the side door, caught his eye, and beckoned to the judge. He went and chatted to his friend for half an hour, returned into court quite another person, saw through the whole case, and made his judgment accordingly. The mental relief, as he described it, was marvellous. And what does my reader suppose formed the topic of conversation that gave such repose to his over-taxed mind? Nothing more than the state of health, &c., of some favourite dogs and horses two hundred miles away.

Men in general may be said to wander through life just as boys scramble through an unexplored wood in search of blackberries, taking their chance of what they may fall upon, or what may befal them. Such individuals are not amongst the gross, ignorant, or sottish beings of society. But there are men who well know the physical machinery of this fair earth, and that fixed laws of Divine government and appointment regulate the whole mechanism, and yet they appear ignorant of the moral machinery within their own bodies, which actuates every movement of their nature, whether in their organic and mental life, or in their animal and bodily life. The celebrated Dr. Samuel Johnson was an instance of this strange inconsistency. He remarks that "in his own person he had had a very severe and alarming instance of the bad effects of too great muscular action, occasioned by a habit of walking too fast. After a day and night of unusual fatigue and rapid pedestrian exertion, together with considerable mental anxiety, I was suddenly seized with an intermission of the pulse at irregular periods. During each intermission I felt the heart give a kind of struggle, as it were, and strike with great violence against the ribs, accompanied by a pecu-liar and most distressing sensation in the cardiac region, which I cannot describe. These symptoms became aggravated and lasted for eight weeks, during which I used horse exercise, and kept at home in a horizontal position. At length the heart gradually lost its morbid irritability, and at the end of fourteen or fifteen weeks I could walk as well as ever."

A medical gentleman who had been on the continent during the greater part of his life, once consulted me on the state of his chest. He was under medical observation upwards of two years, during the whole of which time he only complained of slight cough. But the most extraordinary part of the case was the state of the heart. This organ did not beat at all in the popular sense of the word, but its action consisted rather in a series of rolling, tumbling, intermittent movements, resembling the interrupted and irregular actions of a muscle under the influence of an electro-galvanic battery. This singular state of the circulation was ascertained to have arisen from his having taken, whilst at Berlin, small and increasing doses of Belladonna (Deadly Night-shade), for the purpose of watching its effects. When he arrived at a dose of two grains he became delirious, lost consciousness, and was very ill for several weeks. He was certain that his heart beat regularly before he left England.

The prophylactic influence of Belladonna in preserving the system from scarlet-fever was much extolled about this period, and it was even asserted, by the advocates for its use, that the exemption from scarlatina is as certain in those who take this drug, as the preserva-tive influence of cow-pox, by vaccination, is in warding off the contagion of small-pox.

A striking instance of the long-continued daily action of Bella-donna has just come under the writer's notice. A gentleman with cataract of one eye, and who is totally blind in the other, has used the extract for twenty-five years, and on Sunday last he was enabled, as usual, to read the ordinary print of his Bible, in a quarter of an hour after dropping in the solution of this powerful drug. The effect of it usually continues till after mid-day.

The salutary effects of some kinds of exercise when judiciously employed are very marked in elderly persons, who are unable to use much out-door exertion. An excellent friend of mine, a septuagenarian, suffers from hernia, and is unable to follow his favourite recreation of riding; but, by employing his arms in various calisthenic movements, the chest is expanded, the liver and stomach glow, and the whole body is revived by the stimulus thus given to the circulation.

The writer has seen a few instances of unequivocal diseases of the heart and its great blood-vessel (the aorta) in young men, since the erection of the gymnasium in Regent's Park. A vain desire to perform feats and to surmount difficulties at the serious risk of injuring the health, by those who are not strongly developed in their frame, has defeated the otherwise salutary benefits of judicious gymnastic exercises.

But, since the juvenile fashion of smoking has increased in our large towns, out-door exercise has degenerated. The tobacco trade never flourished so well as at the present time, and never did society present such a mass of sickly, effeminate beings as in the great smokers of the day. Indigestion, or mal-assimilation of food, feeble appetite, misty brains, and an emasculated frame, are the *sequelæ* of over indulgence in the use of this other member of the " Deadly Nightshade " family (Solanaceæ).

SEVENTH STAGE.

OLD MEN.

SEVENTY TO NINETY-EIGHT YEARS.

CHAPTER XVII.

Rapid Fortunes, with Broken-down Constitutions—Endemics and Epidemics—Death in Air, Water, and Walls—Influenza, Cholera, &c.

A MAN, born of healthy parents, and therefore possessed of a sound constitution, may be calculated upon to live seventy years, or upwards, under favourable circumstances. We all know that existence as to duration, is the most uncertain, whilst death is the most certain of all things. The conditions unfavourable to life, come into operation, even in the silent womb. They continue in operation throughout the whole of its appointed period, so that out of a given hundred thousand, a certain proportion are cut off in the first, second, third, &c., years; a comparatively small number attain the full age which nature promises to a sound life, maintained under favourable conditions. Female life is of longer duration than male. The suicidal method of living adopted by a large mass of our fellow-men in this, and other great commercial cities, is growing more and more serious :—a rapid fortune is sought to be made at all hazards, men are impelled forward in business, or in profession, at an incredible speed, a monetary frenzy seizes the mind, and on they madly rush until the over-taxed brain suddenly breaks down, or the finest constitution is quickly ruined. To get to the counting-house or bank at nine, and spend eight or more hours without food or relaxation, is a common practice among the Londoners and Lancashire men. The " go-a-head " system keeps them on the stretch, and after a hurried meal, even then, *business* must be attended to. It has been well said, that " if nature were to punish the daily transgression by the nightly suffering, we should find few who, for the sake of pecuniary gain, would thus expose themselves to misery. But unfortunately, she runs long accounts with her children, and, like a cheating attorney, seldom tenders her bill, till the whole subject of litigation has been eaten up. Paralysis at fifty comes like the *mesne* process upon the victim of commercial enthusiasm, and either hurries him off to that prison from which there is no liberation, or leaves him for a few years, organically alive to *enjoy* the fruits of his labour." * The truth of the above remark has been sadly proved under the writer's notice within these few months. He was summoned soon after daybreak in the summer, to go to the outskirts of London and visit a gentleman seriously ill. He found the patient to be a man in active business in town, about thirty-five years of age, muscular, well-formed, and apparently, with a very healthy constitution. But, alas! he was now prostrate with a sudden attack of epileptiform seizures, totally unconscious, and exhibiting some of the worst features of irreparable damage to the mental powers. The history of this melancholy case, was one of every day occurrence in London and other great towns. He had embarked in active business, and to carry this on more effectually, he had converted the whole town-house into offices, &c., and removed his family, consisting of an amiable lady of thirty, with four children, &c., to the house in question. Here he had lately been privileged, as he said, with a district " letter pillar; " and after his return home from business, he would spend the whole evening, until after midnight, in writing to his various correspondents, and posting them

* Chambers on " Mental Exercise."

before five a.m., for the morning "down" mails. Confusion of thought, a frontal headache, slight indigestion, were the precursors of the fatal blow. In four days from his first seizure, he was removed from earth, leaving his young wife (*enceinte*) and family, to deplore his untimely end and their loss. His mind never recovered itself, only to recognise one or two familiar faces.

But if we reverse this picture, and look at the pursuits of some of our fellow-men, we shall find that sickness and a maudlin state of the mind, are engendered by those whose professions take in a very limited range of objects ; such as country clergymen, retired tradesmen or annuitants, &c., so that by disuse, the brain falls from its original tone, and the results are, sluggishness of body, and feebleness of mind. The education of such persons has only given them an opportunity of employing one or two of the lesser powers of the mind, while all that could have engaged the reflective powers has been omitted. This social error in the education of the mind is at no time felt more keenly than as age advances, and bodily exertion becomes a task. Such persons, especially females, spend their lives in unbroken seclusion, and are content to limit themselves to the performance of a few domestic duties. Motives for exertion, or for exercising the medium of usefulness to others are wanting. They fix their thoughts on themselves—excessive self-love engenders self-pity, and a few narrow and puerile ideas, occupy their minds until they approach a state bordering on insanity; or else they have recourse to stimulating liquors, and thus become a constant source of trouble, if not a disgrace to the circle in which they have moved.

But there are other calamities intimately connected with injuries to our health, which are quite within our control, and therefore, capable of prevention. Fever, ague, scarlatina, erysipelas, and some other formidable diseases, are but expressions of vitiated conditions of the air breathed, just as lead, copper or arsenic poisons may be the result of the contaminated water we drink, of the pickles and preserves we eat, or of the pretty green papers we put on our walls. The wholesale poisoning of a large number of children, which the writer witnessed a short time ago from eating the sweet ornaments of a twelfth-cake (arsenite of copper), is no less serious, or less preventible, than is the fearful havoc that typhus or scarlet fever will make in a dirty, ill-drained slum in London or elsewhere.* Let these conditions be reformed, in accordance with the laws ordained by Providence for human weal, and the diseases vanish. The medical officer of health for the parish of Marylebone observes, that " It is impossible to express in too strong terms, the baneful influence of decomposing excrementitious matters detained in proximity to human habitations;" he then cites two striking in-stances of diseases produced under such influence, and which the author had communicated to him. A room had been fitted up in the Middlesex Hospital, ten years ago, on the basement in the east wing, as a dormitory for nurses. No sooner had they taken pos-session of the sleeping apartment, than the occupants became sickly ; diarrhœa, which proved fatal in two instances, neuralgia of the head and face, rheumatism and erysipelas, being the predominating mala-dies. As no such complaints attacked the nurses in other parts of the building, new dormitories were fitted up elsewhere, and the nurses who were removed thither, were no longer subject to such affections. But the cause was soon afterwards discovered, when this part of the establishment was in process of re-building, two large cesspools were sunk in the earth directly under the floor of the dormitory. These were emptied and filled up, not without giving rise to more attacks of diarrhœa. This room, and an adjoining one, has now been used twelve years, as a laundry and sleeping-room, and the occupants have enjoyed as good health as any other servants of the charity.

* It may be in the recollection of my readers, that the late ex-king of France and family, whilst at Claremont, were seriously ill from the effects of the action of pure spring water upon a newly-faced leaden tank. One of our eminent toxicologists, collected lately 200 grains of dust from the bookshelves of a gentleman's library, who had recently covered the walls with the elegant " French green " paper, and from this dust he obtained eighty grains of arsenious acid. The exhalations from this new-papered room, had given rise to some alarming symptoms in certain members of the family who occupied it.

Those diseases that are regarded as endemic, that is peculiar to, or specially prevalent in one spot, and arising from local causes, are not to be confounded with epidemic complaints, which are not always under our control, and may depend on some obscure atmospheric cause, not clearly ascertained. An endemic disease, as ague, is not contagious, though another, as typhus is, whilst many epidemics seem to be propagated by atmospheric influences only. The singular notoriety that some of the latter class of diseases have to travel, or migrate from one place to another, is generally considered to be connected with a particular state, or contamination of the air.

" On the 3rd of April, 1833," observes Dr. Watson, " all London was smitten with influenza. On the same day ' the Stag ' was coming up the channel, and arrived at two o'clock off Berry Head, on the Devonshire coast; all on board being at that time well. In half an hour afterwards, the breeze being easterly, and blowing off the land, forty men were down with influenza, by six o'clock the number was increased to sixty, and by two o'clock the next day, to 160; on the self-same evening, a regiment on duty, at Portsmouth, was in a perfectly healthy state ; but, by the next morning, so many of the soldiers of that regiment were affected by ' influenza,' that the garrison duty could not be performed by it." The impossibility of accounting for its prevalence, upon the principle of mere contagion, is greater than the explanation of its outbreak being due to some peculiar vitiation of the air. The curious behaviour of another epidemic, erysipelas, is also worthy of record. For several years this disease constantly occurred in an accident ward on the ground-floor of the west wing of the Middlesex Hospital (five cases within a very brief period). The ward is the largest in the establishment, and therefore deficiency of breathing space, a common exciter of erysipelas, was scarcely to be suspected as the cause of the malady. By careful observation, it was noticed that the occupants of the beds, most liable to be affected, were directly over the dust-hole of the hospital, which was situated in a vault in the western front area ; the effluvia from which escaped, and entered the ward by the window. By properly securing the dust-hole with double doors, and by fastening the ward window so that it could never be opened, the further noxious exhalations were prevented. Four years elapsed, and not one case of the disease occurred ; when, suddenly, it again manifested itself in the same beds. The outer door of the dust-hole was found off its hinges, and the exhalations again escaped. The door was repaired, and the disease is unknown in the ward ever since as a sporadic complaint.

" There are many facts," observes an eminent writer, on ventilation,* " to show that the impurity of retained breath, scarcely heeded in general, has been the chief element of the foul atmosphere which has led to cholera outbreaks." Tooting parish school, with its 1,000 inmates, of which 300 were suddenly attacked, and the Taunton Union house, were remarkable examples. In the latter, thirty cases occurred amongst the girls, in whose room the glass windows were entire, whereas in the boys' room, where panes of glass were broken, and fresh air admitted, not a single case occurred ; and there was only one other case in the town.

Man should learn, that with the same mechanical certainty that he can substitute the pure water of a passing tide, or river stream, for defiled water near the shore, so he may substitute pure air from the atmosphere, for any air near him that has become unfit for his use, and thus ward off diseases of a deadly nature and preserve himself in comparative health. In the metropolis, it is computed that amongst linen-drapers, haberdashers, and similar trades in hosiery, &c., no fewer than ten thousand shopmen are annually draughted into this work, from the provincial factories, &c., to replace a similar number who are compelled to leave London on account of ill-health, from over confinement in close, ill-ventilated shops ; if they can get over the first two years' residence, they are so far acclimatized that they enjoy tolerable health afterwards, though many ultimately fall early victims to consumption.

Every person suffering from a contagious disease becomes a

* Dr. Arnott.

"nidus," from whence it may spread. The noxious particles emanating from the body mix with other animal gases thrown off. But as there is no liquid poison which may not be rendered harmless by copious dilution with fresh water, so there can be no aerial poison, the action of which may not be similarly influenced by dilution with fresh air. The exhalations from animal bodies, in health or in disease, are always specifically heavier than the upper strata of air, and they are, therefore, confined to the lower parts of the room, where, like oil floating on water, with pure air above, they stagnate until copious streams of cold and lighter air glide along the floor, and drive the aerial poison to the chimney flues, or windows, whilst it thus becomes so diluted as to be rendered innocuous.

The nation is at this moment wrapt in universal gloom. The beloved Queen of our realms is a widow, and her amiable and universally loved Consort has been taken from us by the hand of death, through typhoid fever (the twenty-one-day fever of our forefathers), the product of an animal poison. He inhaled it in some secret and mysterious way on the first or second day of this month (December), and on the 15th day the people of Great Britain were called to weep over the loss of one who, next to our own beloved Sovereign, was revered, nay, caressed by all classes of society. In the flower of his age and the fulness of his strength, in all the glow and vigour of manhood, it has pleased the Almighty Disposer of life and of death to take from amongst us Prince Albert, a hardy, abstemious man of forty-two. May we reverently bow down to this national calamity, and hear the still small voice replying to every inquiring thought, " Be still, and know that I am God."

FINIS.

W. H. Collingridge, City Press, 117 to 119, Aldersgate Street, London, E.C.

www.ingramcontent.com/pod-product-compliance
Lightning Source LLC
Chambersburg PA
CBHW032203010726
47493CB00008BA/2802